CINEMA

POOL

ICE RINK

NS

LIBRARY

ELF VILLAGE

NS

PUFFIN BOOKS

THE CHRISTMASAURUS

Also by Tom Fletcher, written with Dougie Poynter,
for younger readers:

THE DINOSAUR THAT POOPED CHRISTMAS

THE DINOSAUR THAT POOPED A PLANET!

THE DINOSAUR THAT POOPED THE PAST!

THE DINOSAUR THAT POOPED THE BED!

THE DINOSAUR THAT POOPED A RAINBOW!

THE DINOSAUR THAT POOPED DADDY!

THE DINOSAUR THAT POOPED A LOT!
(written specially for World Book Day 2015)

THE CHRISTMASAURUS

TOM FLETCHER

Illustrations by Shane Devries

PUFFIN

PUFFIN BOOKS

UK | USA | Canada | Ireland | Australia
India | New Zealand | South Africa

Puffin Books is part of the Penguin Random House group of companies
whose addresses can be found at global.penguinrandomhouse.com.

www.penguin.co.uk   www.puffin.co.uk   www.ladybird.co.uk

First published 2016
008

Cover, illustrations, text and 'I Ho, Ho, Hope It's Santa' lyrics
copyright © Tom Fletcher, 2016
Illustrations by Shane Devries

The moral right of the author and illustrator has been asserted

Set in Baskerville MT Pro
Text design by Mandy Norman
Printed in Great Britain by Clays Ltd, St Ives plc

A CIP catalogue record for this book is available from the British Library

HARDBACK
ISBN: 978–0–141–37332–4

INTERNATIONAL PAPERBACK
ISBN: 978–0–141–37791–9

All correspondence to:
Puffin Books, Penguin Random House Children's
80 Strand, London WC2R 0RL

For Buzz and Buddy.
Merry Christmas, my little elves.

You are about to have an ADVENTURE with:

A boy called **William Trundle**.

His dad,
Mr Bob Trundle.

Santa.

Lots of **elves**.

Brenda Payne
the meanest girl in the school
(possibly the world).

A very nasty piece of work
called the **Hunter** and his
dog **Growler**.

And, of course, a
dinosaur called the
Christmasaurus!

CONTENTS

THE END OF THE DINOSAURS

This story starts like all good stories do, *a long time ago*. Not just a long time ago, but a very, *very*, **very** long time ago. Squillions of years ago, in fact. Long before your granny and your granddad were born. Before there were any human beings at all. Before cars and aeroplanes, even before there was the internet, there was something even better . . .

DINOSAURS!

Dinosaurs were the most awesome creatures ever to walk the planet. There were lots of them, and they came in all shapes and sizes. There were small ones that were not much bigger than dogs or cats, some with spiky prickle horns on their backs. There were stupendously ginormous ones called Seismosaurus that were longer than five double-decker buses, with necks thicker than tree trunks and skin like the hard rubber tyres of a tractor. I know that sounds hard to believe, but it's definitely true, because this is a book and books don't lie.

I'd like to tell you about two very special dinosaurs. We'll call them Mumosaurus and Dadlodocus (those weren't their real names, of course – that would just be silly).

Mumosaurus and Dadlodocus had been out all day in the hot, hot heat of the prehistoric sun, and were returning home to their tidy little nest. But what they found in its place was something horrendously horrible: an almighty pile of rocks, bones and dust. Their home had been raided by evil scavenger dinosaurs, and these sneaky, scroungy little scavengers had smashed up their home good and proper!

But for Mumosaurus and Dadlodocus the mess was

the last thing on their minds, because they had left their most precious things alone inside the nest: twelve dinosaur *eggs*, which were now nowhere to be seen!

As you can imagine, Mumosaurus and Dadlodocus were devastated. They stood in the wreckage of their nest, weeping and roaring for a very long time, until the sun went down and the moon and stars filled the sky above the jungle.

That night, a light breeze was blowing through the enormous trees and a sliver of silvery moonlight found its way to the remains of the nest. Suddenly, something caught Dadlodocus's eye. Something smooth and shiny was reflecting a moonbeam from under a pile of bones and mud. He quickly and gently lifted the rocks and rubble, and there it was, gleaming, perfectly unharmed in the moonlight.

It was their one last **EGG**.

How this one and only egg had escaped the hungry scavengers' rampage was a mystery. Perhaps their greedy tummies were full up, or maybe this egg had rolled out of sight when they were smashing and crushing the others. Whatever the reason, all that mattered was that

Mumosaurus and Dadlodocus had one egg left. The tiny dinosaur that was curled up safely inside that egg became the most important thing in the world to them, and they weren't going to let anything bad happen to it ever again!

But something bad *was* about to happen – something that would change the world for ever.

Something **big**.

Something **astronomically, intergalactically, outer spacey-wacey big!**

The pearly moonlight that blanketed the dinosaurs' broken nest suddenly seemed to turn yellow. Then the yellow turned orange and then to a hot, fiery red. Mumosaurus and Dadlodocus peeped out from their

home, staring in disbelief. It was as though the moon itself was on fire!

As they watched, the whole sky turned into a violent firework display of whizzing hot rocks and shooting stars – and not the kind of shooting stars that you and I know, which swoosh prettily over the sky like beautiful little scratches of light in space. These ones didn't swoosh by at all. These ones smashed straight down like red-hot thunderbolts that exploded into thousands of fireballs as they hit the Earth!

Panic and chaos consumed the jungle. Flaming trees were uprooted by huge, five-double-decker-bus-sized dinosaurs, and smaller dinosaurs were squished and trampled. The night sky was brighter than the lightest day, and the moon felt hotter than the midday sun – but there was only one thing on Mumosaurus's and Dadlodocus's minds.

Protecting their egg!

They *had* to get their egg to safety!

So they ran. They ran as fast as their dinosaur feet could carry them, desperately clinging on to that last, treasured egg. They joined the stampede of thousands of terrified dinosaurs fleeing the danger, but no matter how fast and how far they ran they couldn't seem to escape. After all, how can you run from the sky?

Mumosaurus and Dadlodocus were swept away into the crowd, pulled this way and pushed that way in a

great sea of dinosaurs, and, as hard as they tried, they just couldn't hold on to their egg any longer!

It slipped from their grip and fell to the ground.

Now, I bet you're thinking that the egg was crushed instantly, right? Well – smartyclogs cleverpants – it wasn't, actually!

A pile of leaves broke the egg's fall, and it rolled into the stampede, unharmed. It was kickerbashed and knockerboshed every which way – but it *still* didn't crack! Mumosaurus and Dadlodocus chased after it as it bounced in between giant diplodocus legs and rolled under stomping stegosaurus feet, narrowly avoiding being squished time after time. It rolled and rolled, as

if it had a mind of its own, falling from rocky ledges to treetops and swooshing down slushy mudslides, as Mumosaurus and Dadlodocus chased desperately after it.

If Mumosaurus and Dadlodocus had been looking up at the sky instead of trying to find their egg, they would have seen such a terrifyingly, heart-stoppingly, frighteningly scary sight. The whole sky was on fire above them. What they had thought was the flaming moon was, in fact, a whopping, giganterrific, planet-smasher of a meteorite. It had travelled from the deepest depths of space, and was about to smash-whack into Planet Earth and wipe out all the dinosaurs for ever!

But just before the meteor did its planet smashing, the lucky egg rolled all the way to the edge of a tall, jagged cliff, high above the ferocious ocean. All Mumosaurus and Dadlodocus could do was watch helplessly as their last precious egg, with their tiny baby dinosaur inside, calmly toppled over the edge of the cliff and out of sight.

Gone for ever.

The egg fell straight down, missing the rocky face of the cliff by millimetres. This was a very lucky egg indeed!

PROLOGUE

It plopped peacefully into the ocean below, like a pebble in a lake, and instantly sank deep into the darkness, leaving the fiery chaos of the world above the waves. Eventually it came to rest on a soft, sheltered spot on the ocean floor, as the meteor shower it left behind rained down unforgivingly, destroying every living dinosaur on the planet.

Except one.

The one inside the egg!

While the egg lay peacefully at the bottom of the ocean, the world continued to burn – and then it froze solid, in an ice age that would last for thousands of years.

There the egg remained, deep in the ice, frozen in time, just waiting to be discovered . . .

CHAPTER ONE

WILLIAM TRUNDLE

This is William Trundle.

There's something you should know about William: William liked dinosaurs. Actually, he didn't just like them. He *loved* them. In fact, he loved them so much I should probably write it in big letters like this . . .

WILLIAM LOVED DINOSAURS!
WILLIAM HAD . . . sorry,

William had dinosaur pyjamas, dinosaur socks, dinosaur pants, a dinosaur-shaped toothbrush, dinosaur wallpaper, two dinosaur posters, a dinosaur lampshade and more dinosaur toys than he could fit into a bag for life, but if there was one thing William knew for sure, it was that you could never have too many dinosaur toys!

William lived in a wonky little house on the edge of a busy town on the edge of a busier city, but even though the house was small it never really felt that way because only two people lived in it: William and his dad, Bob Trundle.

Now, I bet you're wondering why William didn't have a mum. Well, of course he did have a mum once, but sadly she died a long time ago, when William was very young. So it had been just William and Mr Trundle for as long as William could remember.

As well as dinosaurs, William loved **Christmas** – but not half as much as his dad did.

Mr Trundle loved Christmas so much that whenever Christmas Day was over he would sob uncontrollably for a whole week, sometimes until the end of January, desperately clinging on to Christmas! He even had a secret Christmas tree hidden in his wardrobe, which was permanently decorated, and it lit up when he opened the door to get his socks. Each morning as Mr Trundle got dressed he would look at his secret tree and say to himself, 'Every step you take away from last Christmas brings you one step closer to the next.' It was these words that got him through the year.

On this particular morning, though, Mr Trundle was feeling very merry indeed – because it was the first day of December.

'Time to get ready for school, Willypoos!' Mr Trundle called from the kitchen as he spread butter on to two steaming hot crumpets (Mr Trundle's favourite breakfast).

William rolled his eyes at the silly nickname his dad used for him – *Willypoos*!

'Dad, you can't keep calling me that. I'm seven and three quarters. It's embarrassing!' William shouted from his bedroom as he stuffed his schoolbag full of books.

'I thought we'd agreed that I can call you Willypoos when you're not at school? You can't go changing the rules willy-nilly, Willypoos!' Mr Trundle teased as he walked into his son's bedroom. 'Happy first of December!'

Mr Trundle beamed as he placed a breakfast tray down on William's desk and nodded his head excitedly at a rectangular object perched perfectly next to the plate of golden crumpets. William followed his gaze and saw that it was a chocolate-filled Advent calendar.

'Thanks, Dad! Where's yours?' asked William. Every year, William and Mr Trundle would each have an Advent calendar, and open a new door together every morning before school. It was a Trundle tradition.

William thought he saw a flicker of sadness on Mr Trundle's face, which was quickly replaced by a smile.

'I thought it might be fun to share one this year, William,' Mr Trundle said. Lately they'd been sharing a lot of things, as Mr Trundle didn't have very much money. But William didn't mind.

'Oh, OK!' he said. 'I'll open the door and you can have the first chocolate, Dad.'

'How about *I* open the door and *you* have the first chocolate, William?' Mr Trundle suggested.

'Thanks, Dad,' William said, grinning. He'd secretly hoped his dad would say that.

'Say "Cheese"!' said Mr Trundle as he quickly snapped a photo of the two of them. 'Ah, that'll make a lovely Christmas card this year!' he said, admiring the photograph. It was another Trundle tradition to take a photograph on the first of December for the Christmas cards they would send to a long list of their distant relatives: Aunty Kim on the Isle of Wight, Great-Nanna Joan who looked like a witch, cousins Lilly and Joe, Aunty Julie, second cousin Sam, Uncle H. Trundle, Great-Grandpa Ken . . . It was a long list, half of whom William had never met!

'William, have you thought about what you're going to ask Santa for this year? You'll need to write your letter soon,' said Mr Trundle as he peeled open the first door on the Advent calendar. William took out the small snowman-shaped chocolate, but suddenly didn't feel like eating it.

'My dear boy, what on earth's the matter?' asked Mr Trundle.

'Well . . . it's . . . it's just that I don't think Santa can

14

bring me what I want this year,' said William, staring longingly at the dinosaur poster on his wall. 'I'm pretty sure the elves can't make real dinosaurs.'

'Make?' repeated Mr Trundle as he took a knowing sip of his cup of tea. 'The elves don't *make* anything at all!'

William looked very confused. 'But I thought Santa's elves *made* all the presents in the North Pole,' he said.

'PAH!' cried Mr Trundle, spitting out a mouthful of tea. 'Well, William, I'm afraid that's all just a big pile of poppycock, fiddle-faddle, mouth-waffling, gibbery-faff nonsense. Whoever told you that is a complete knobblyplank! *Make* presents? Ha! Would you like me to tell you how elves *really* work, William?' he asked, a sudden sparkle in his eyes.

'Oh, please do, Dad!' William cried, and made himself comfortable. He always loved it when his dad told him stories. He was very good at them – and he was particularly good at Christmas stories, for, as you already know, Mr Trundle loved everything about Christmas. He knew all there was to know about Santa, the elves and the North Pole. Ever since he was a little boy himself, it had been his favourite time of year, and he would always be the first person to start celebrating Christmas. One year, he'd put up their Christmas tree in July (which really annoyed the neighbours). William loved it.

'Well, the first thing you should know is that elf hands are far too small to build any decent sort of toy, and, on top of that, they only have three fingers.'

'Three fingers? No way!' William said, making funny shapes with his own hands, trying to imagine he had three elf fingers. 'How small are elves, Dad?' he asked.

'Very small, William. Looking at an elf is like looking at a human through a pair of binoculars, if you were holding them the wrong way round,' Mr Trundle explained.

'Oh, wow!' said William, who knew exactly what he meant.

'No, the elves aren't toy-makers at all,' Mr Trundle went on. 'There are only two jobs that the North Pole elves are good at: farming and mining. Let me tell you how it works, my boy. First, Santa receives letters from girls and boys from all around the world, just like you, William, asking for all different sorts of Christmas presents. Santa then sits by his fireplace, in his rocking chair, and reads *every* letter aloud. **Not** in his head, William!'

William nodded, listening intently.

'This is very important, William, because in his letter-reading room there is a very old, very crooked, very magical Christmas tree. If you saw it, you would probably think it was a dead twig in a plant pot – but it is very important. It was the very first Christmas tree that ever lived, and it's still alive – and now it sits and listens to Santa read.'

'A tree that *listens*? Really, Dad?' questioned William at this rather absurd-sounding fact.

'Of course! All trees listen, William. Why do you think they're so quiet all the time? They're listening, of course!' said Mr Trundle, making perfect sense. 'As Santa reads the letters aloud, the old, crooked, magical Christmas tree sprouts bunches of very peculiar-looking bean pods.'

'Bean pods!' cried William. 'What on earth are bean pods?'

'They are magical Christmas bean pods, William, and

Santa picks these odd pods and gives them to the farmer elves. The farmer elves boil them in pots until the Christmas beans pop out. These beans are very large, with red and white swirls. If you ate one, William, it would taste so delicious that your eyes would cry rainbows and then fall right out of your head, so they are *never* to be eaten.'

William nodded and made a mental note never to eat a Christmas bean.

'The farmer elves then take the beans out to the purest white snowfields and plant them, deep in the cold, powdery snow. When they're finished, all the elves gather together and wait for a sign. While they wait, they sing a song.'

Mr Trundle cleared his throat and started singing the most peculiar elf song in his best elf voice:

'We're waiting for a sign –
It's taking so much time.
Hurry up, you silly Christmas beans!
We want to go inside!

'Our bogies feel like icicles!
Where is this silly sign?
Hurry up, you slowpoke Christmas beans!
It's nearly Christmastime!'

'Wow!' said William. 'The elves really sing that song?'

'Every year!' said Mr Trundle. 'Then, eventually, when the timing is just right, the sky above the North Pole lights up in a wash of glorious dancing colours.'

'*The Northern Lights?*' yelled William. 'I've seen them on the telly!'

'That's right, son! The beautiful Northern Lights. That's the sign they wait for! That's when the mining elves go to work!'

'And what do the mining elves do?' asked William.

'I'll tell you, my lad,' said Mr Trundle happily. 'They dig, dig, diggedy dig under the snowfields and into the

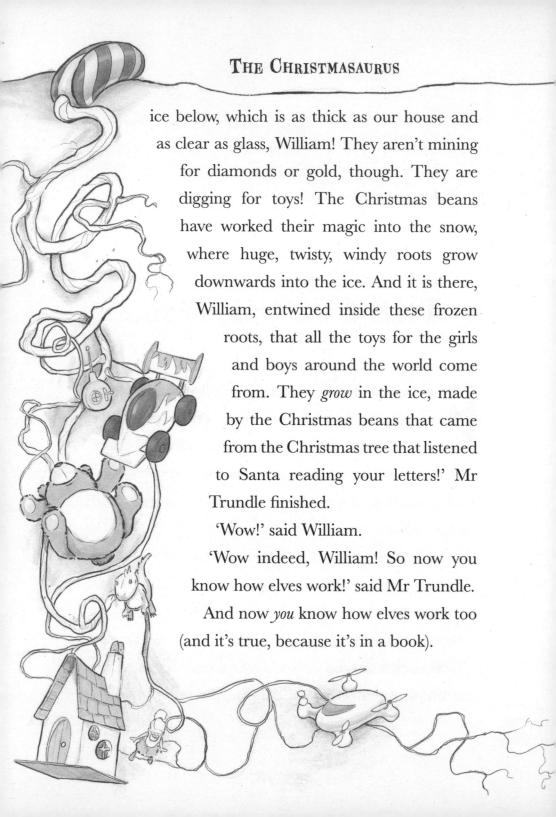

ice below, which is as thick as our house and as clear as glass, William! They aren't mining for diamonds or gold, though. They are digging for toys! The Christmas beans have worked their magic into the snow, where huge, twisty, windy roots grow downwards into the ice. And it is there, William, entwined inside these frozen roots, that all the toys for the girls and boys around the world come from. They *grow* in the ice, made by the Christmas beans that came from the Christmas tree that listened to Santa reading your letters!' Mr Trundle finished.

'Wow!' said William.

'Wow indeed, William! So now you know how elves work!' said Mr Trundle.

And now *you* know how elves work too (and it's true, because it's in a book).

CHAPTER TWO

THE FROZEN EGG

Far away from William's wonky little house, snowflakes were falling from enormous fluffy snow clouds. They were the thickest snowflakes you could ever imagine. If you were to stick out your tongue to catch one in your mouth, you would feel so full up that you wouldn't need to eat any dinner – that's how thick these snowflakes were.

They weren't ordinary snowflakes, because this was the North Pole, and in the North Pole *nothing* is ordinary!

The snowflakes hit the ground with a thud that echoed back from the surrounding mountains like the constant drumming of a marching band:

21

Thud! Thud! Thud!

But that wasn't the only sound that could be heard. If you listened closely, you could hear voices, deep underground, singing together in time with the thudding of the snowflakes. These were the voices of the North Pole elves – the very same ones that Mr Trundle had just told William about.

They were singing their digging song, which went something like this:

> 'Dig diggedy, dig diggedy, dig diggedy diggedy
>   diggedy,
> Dig diggedy, dig diggedy, dig diggedy diggedy dig!
> Oh! The dwarves that dig for diamonds sing hi-ho,
> Hi-ho, hi-ho, hi-ho,
> And the fairies flying high all say hello,
> Hello, hello, hello!
> But we're not fairies or dwarves –
> We're Santa's elves of course!
> And the reason why we're dig, dig, diggedy,

Digging through the snow?
We're digging up toys and games and stuff!
We'll keep on digging though most of us
Can't feel our fingers, can't feel our toes,
But we'll keep dig, digging through the ice
   and snow!'

The elves made up songs like this all the time. In fact, the elves of the North Pole didn't speak normally at all, EVER! They only spoke in rhyme. For example, if a North Pole elf wanted a glass of orange juice, they would never just say, 'Can I have a glass of orange juice, please?' The elf would say something like:

'Can I have some orange juice, please,
Freshly picked and freshly squeezed?
Peel off the skin and pop out the pips
And give me extra juicy bits!'

Or if a North Pole elf were to say good morning to another North Pole elf, they would say:

'Good morning, fellow North Pole elf!
I hope your day brings lots of wealth,
But if it doesn't don't worry yourself –
Be thankful that you've got your health!'

They had rhymes and songs for every occasion and were making new ones up all the time. Some were rather good, and others were awful – but they would sing them just the same.

On this particularly chilly December day of digging, there were eight elves out in the ice mines underneath the snowfields of the North Pole. Their names were: Snozzletrump, Specklehump, Sparklefoot, Sugarsnout, Starlump, Spudcheeks, Snowcrumb and Sprout. They were very small, just as Mr Trundle had said, only

about as tall as your left knee, and they all wore the most wonderfully peculiar clothes, from dresses made of teacups to fluffy coats covered in Northern Lightbulbs. They were quite a spectacular sight.

Every elf had a different but equally important job.

Snozzletrump dug the hole.

Specklehump held the lantern so that Snozzletrump could see.

Sparklefoot lit a fire.

Sugarsnout boiled the kettle.

Starlump made the tea.

Spudcheeks toasted four crumpets (half a crumpet for each elf).

Snowcrumb buttered the crumpets.

Sprout kept watch.

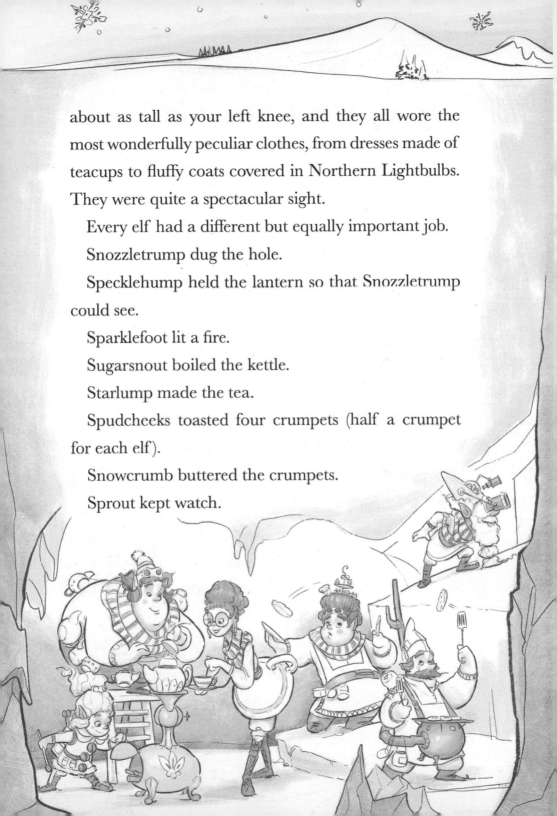

They had been digging holes, eating crumpets and drinking tea all morning and were starting to think about lunch (North Pole elves were very small, but were always very hungry).

'We've no more crumpets left to munch!' said Sprout. 'I'm hungry, let's go back for lunch.'

But Snozzletrump wasn't listening. Snozzletrump was inside a long tunnel he'd been digging in the ice for the past two hours. He was deep in thought and lost in the song he was singing to himself:

> 'I've been digging through snow and ice
> For many days and countless nights,
> So that every girl and every boy
> Gets a special Christmas . . . EGG?'

There was a great gasp from all the elves. Spudcheeks even dropped his half crumpet in the snow, buttered side down!

'That *line* didn't *rhyme*!' chimed Snowcrumb from the back of the concerned group. It was very rare that a North Pole elf would ever *not* rhyme.

The Frozen Egg

'I seem to have *found* something strange in the . . . *ground*!' yelled Snozzletrump, coming back to his rhyming senses.

The seven elves outside the tunnel dropped their tea and crumpets at once and rushed forward to take a look. Specklehump adjusted the great brass lantern he was carrying on a long pole so that it shone its light over their heads. The ice tunnel lit up in great blues and yellows, and what the elves saw left them all completely gobble-mouthed, pokey-eyed, wonky-brained and confused.

It was an enormous frozen egg!

Most of the elves were more than two hundred years old and had seen all sorts of weird, wacky things in the North Pole, but never ever had any of them seen an egg frozen in the ice.

They started whispering and gossiping to each other (in rhyme, obviously), trying to get a better peep at the beautiful shiny shell of the egg, which was stuck halfway out of the ice. As they all nudged closer, there was such a kerfuffle that an argument broke out between Sugarsnout and Snozzletrump, which to you and me would have sounded like a rather chirpy duet. It went a little like this:

'There's an EGG under the snow!'
'How did it get here?'
'I don't know!'
'Well, dig it up, let's take it back!'
'Dig it up? But it might crack!'
'We can't just leave it stuck in the ice –
We could cook it for dinner . . . It might taste nice!'
'Cook it? COOK IT? You can't do that!
There's something inside it waiting to hatch!'

Just as Snozzletrump finished singing his line, something happened that made all the elves jump.

The egg *wobbled*!

There was a great silence in the tunnel as the elves huddled together, staring at the egg. There was something inside it, all right! Something *alive*! Then all at once, as if they had been planning this routine for months, the elves started singing together in perfect unison:

'Dig up the egg –
Let's take it back!
Dig up the egg,
So it can hatch!
Dig up the egg,
So we can find
What sort of thing's
Alive inside!
A frozen fish?
A chilly chicken?
Santa will know.
So let's start digging!'

All eight elves worked together to carefully dig out the egg. It was a tricky, fiddly business that only North Pole elves could do. If humans had found the egg, it would have been squish-flattened like a pancake! But the elves were gentle, expert diggers. Sugarsnout used the steam from the pot of tea to melt the most solidly frozen layer of ice. Snowcrumb used his buttery crumpet knife to gently chip away pieces of ice from around the egg. Starlump brushed away the loose snow, while Sprout hopped up and down excitedly, shouting encouraging rhymes to help (with a mouthful of crumpet, of course). After only fifteen minutes and twenty-two seconds, the stuck egg popped free from the ice.

All the elves took their wonderfully thick coats and scarves, and wrapped them around the giant egg. It was taller than an elf standing on another elf's shoulders, fatter than three elves and heavier than all eight of the elves put together.

THE FROZEN EGG

It took a great effort for them to carry it, but if there's one thing elves are good at, it's teamwork.

They all bunched together with the freezing North Pole wind *whooshing* over their cold arms, and they carried that frozen egg out of the ice mines, over the snowfields, and took it to the wisest person they knew.

The only person who would know what to do with a frozen egg in the North Pole.

Santa!

CHAPTER THREE
SANTA'S BOTTOM

Have you ever seen a house that's bigger than a school? Santa's house is.

Have you ever seen a house that's bigger than a castle? Santa's house is.

Have you ever seen a house that's bigger than the moon?

OK – Santa's house isn't quite that big. But it *is* pretty

massive!

In your head, imagine the biggest, grandest house you've ever seen. Now imagine it's all made of strong, sturdy wood, like a giant log cabin. Now add a huge twisty turret, four tall chimney pots puffing out clouds of glittery smoke, and ninety-nine windows of brightly coloured glass (and one frosted one, for Santa's bathroom).

Now imagine an enormous front door made of thick, chunky pine, with a gleaming door knocker shaped like a snowflake made of solid, unbreakable ice. Leading to the door, there *used* to be a knobbly cobblestone path, but it was so hard for the elves to walk on that Santa had it replaced with a toboggan run. Now the elves zoom down to the front door on miniature sledges.

On either side of the toboggan run, imagine a sprawling garden, jam-packed full of snow-covered Christmas trees.

This is the North Pole Snow Ranch.

It's where Santa lives, right at the centre of the North Pole.

Snozzletrump and the others lived very close by: at the top of the toboggan run path was the elf city (which was about the size of a small human village). There were large stables for the reindeer, with triple-height ceilings so they could fly inside. A Christmas-themed miniature-golf course. A cinema showing all the greatest Christmas films. A library (full of Christmas stories). Four North Star-bucks coffee shops. An ice-skating rink (which was really just Santa's permanently

frozen outdoor swimming pool). Because elves love food so much, especially sweet things, every other shop was either a sweet shop or a bakery, so the air always smelt of warm sugar and fresh crumpets. And there was so much more! Here's a little map so you can see . . .

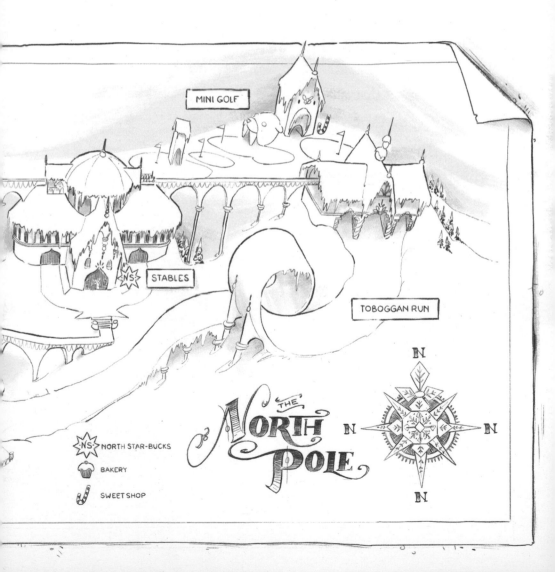

MINI GOLF

STABLES

TOBOGGAN RUN

THE NORTH POLE

N

N   N

N

NS NORTH STAR-BUCKS

BAKERY

SWEET SHOP

It was a fantastic place to live.

Suddenly, Snozzletrump, Specklehump, Sparklefoot, Sugarsnout, Starlump, Spudcheeks, Snowcrumb and Sprout burst in through the enormous wooden front doors of the Snow Ranch. They waddled into the entrance hall, hunched together under the weight of the frozen egg on their backs.

**'Santa! Come quick!
Santa! Come help!
This egg is too heavy
For North Pole elves!'**

the eight elves cried out.

All of a sudden the **BOOM, BOOM** of heavy boot steps rattled around the entrance hall where the eight egg-finders waited. Then the footsteps stopped and there was silence for a moment. Out of nowhere, a huge, heavy man crashed down from the ceiling on a circus trapeze!

It was Santa – he always liked to make an entrance!

He was the largest man you could ever imagine.

Imagine your two fattest relatives (it's OK – they won't know you thought of them). Now imagine that those two people were one person! Yep, *that's* how big Santa was – not just fat, but **fat-tastic!**

He was easily the size of fifty elves put together, but for a man of such enormous proportions Santa was surprisingly nimble.

He was the fastest runner in the northern hemisphere.

He could dance on the tips of his toes like a ballerina.

He could backflip and somersault like a giant, stealthy ninja.

He once tightrope-walked from the North Pole to the South Pole . . . and halfway back again (he had to get a lift home on the sleigh because of a nasty blister)!

Santa triple backflipped into a double forward roll across the vast entrance hall and came to an abrupt stop millimetres away from the group of elves, his deep red onesie stretched tightly over his round belly. He hopped, skipped and tippy-toed around them, peering excitedly at what they were carrying on their backs, still hidden under their woolly elf coats.

'How *exciting*!' Santa said giddily. 'How jolly *marvellous*.

Spiffing! *Oh*, what a funderful sight. *Oh*, what a wonder. How puzzlingly mysterious. How mysteriously puzzling. You eight little elfywelfies, what have you here? Can I touch it? Shall we look? *Why*, I know what this is, of course! It's obvious. This is a . . . it's a . . . What *is* it?'

With that, the elves pulled off their coats and scarves and revealed the shimmery shell of the enormous egg.

'*Hmmmm!*' Santa said curiously.

'*Hmmmmmmmm!*' the elves repeated.

'Interesting . . .' Santa whispered through his thick white whiskery and twisty moustache.

'*Very* interesting . . .' the elves replied, hoping Santa would next say something that rhymed.

'And where was it . . . *nesting*?' Santa asked, looking rather impressed with himself at managing to find a rhyme. He was usually absolutely rotten at rhyming with the elves, which they found extremely frustrating.

'In the ice! It was frozen! It's lucky that it wasn't broken!' cried out Sprout.

'Crikey!' Santa said, looking rather concerned all of a sudden. 'If this egg has been frozen down in the ice mines, then it must be very old. Even older than me, and I'm five hundred and . . . no, six hundred and fifty . . . twenty . . . *Jollygosh!* I seem to have forgotten how old I am!'

The elves all looked at each other, half excited by the riddle of the old frozen egg, and half concerned that Santa had now started talking with absolutely no concern for rhythm or rhyme.

'What do we do with an egg that's frozen?' asked Sparklefoot.

'Boil it up or crack it open?' answered Spudcheeks.

Just then the egg gave another little wibbly wobble!

'Boil it up? Crack it open?' Santa cried. 'You barmy bunch of tiny twerps, we can't do that! There's something inside this egg. Something *alive*! This egg needs to be warmed slowly. Cared for. *Loved*. This egg needs its mother to sit on it, like a mother hen sits on her eggs.' He looked around the room as if hoping to see some sort of giant hen that could sit on the egg to warm it up.

'But, Santa, this egg has no mum! It needs someone else's bum!' said Snozzletrump, who tried to use words like *bum* or *bottom* as much as possible.

'Golly jingle bells, you're right, Snozzletrump!' said Santa. 'But whose bottom is big enough to warm up this frozen egg?'

And with that the elves broke into a song that went something like this:

'This egg needs warming under someone's bum,
But an elf's backside is a tiny one.
If every elf put its bottom on the egg,
The egg would freeze their bums instead.

'So an elf can't do it – that's a silly idea!
An elf can't do it – it would take a whole year!
If an elf can't do it, there must be someone else,
Someone much bigger than a North Pole elf!'

And the elves finished their song and dance on their knees, pointing their fingers at Santa, looking up at him with hopeful eyes.

'Me?' Santa said. '*I* can't sit on that egg! It's almost Christmastime – there's so much planning to be done . . . and . . . packing and . . . wrapping . . .' Santa hesitated, but deep down he knew what needed to be done – and he knew that *he* was the only person to do it. His elves would take care of all the Christmas preparations. All he needed to do was park his giant, jolly, warm bottom on top of that frozen egg!

So that's exactly what he did!

CHAPTER FOUR

INSIDE THE EGG

S anta sat on the egg day and night. It was very uncomfortable, as I'm sure you can imagine, but the elves made him breakfast, brunch, elevensies, lunch, tea, dinner and supper every day, and delivered it to him on a tray (with a song). They even wheeled his television into the makeshift egg-warming room, the airing cupboard, so that Santa could watch his favourite Christmas films (which were mostly about him!) whilst the egg defrosted beneath his enormous backside.

Occasionally the egg would wobble a little, and the longer Santa perched on top of it, the more and more it wobbled! Santa knew this was a good sign that his warm bottom was doing the trick.

But time was not on the egg's side. Each day that passed brought Christmas a day closer.

'Come on, egg-wobbler, whatever you are. If you don't get a shift on and hatch by Christmas Eve, then I'll have no choice but to fly off and leave you! I'd hate to give up on you, but the children need me. It's my duty, y'see,' Santa whispered worriedly, as the clock struck midnight, signalling the end of another no-show day from whatever was inside the egg.

At that moment, Santa had an idea. Maybe the egg would hatch faster if the airing cupboard was even warmer.

'Snozzletrump, whack up the central heating to full blast at once!' Santa ordered.

After a few hours, the ranch felt like a sauna. Sprout even cut the legs off his trousers and turned them into shorts. It wasn't long before all the elves thought that was a pretty nifty idea and followed suit, and for the first time in history the North Pole gift shop in the elf city started selling sweater vests instead of sweaters, and snapback caps instead of thick woolly elf hats. It was the hottest Santa's ranch had ever been! Santa stripped right down to his stripy red and white undervest and his best Christmas underpants (the red ones with white snowflakes on them that played 'Jingle Bells' when you pulled them up). He was so hot and sticky, but he didn't mind. He would do whatever it took to get that *thing* inside the egg out safely.

All this time, Santa and the elves had been trying to guess what was wobbling around inside the egg. Some elves guessed it was a bunch of big bunnies, others thought it would be a large polar bear. There were lots of stupid nonsensical elf guesses and none of them got it right.

But of course, *they* hadn't read the start of this story as *you* have. I'm sure you've guessed by now that this egg was the exact same special egg I told you about at the beginning – so, unlike Santa and the elves, you know *exactly* what was inside it . . .

Soon there was only one chocolate left in Santa's Advent calendar – and that meant it was Christmas Eve.

'Come on, Eggy, there's not much time!' sighed Santa, patting the smooth shell under his bottom.

All the North Pole elves and their families had crowded into the egg-warming room to show their support. Some had brought candles. Others had brought little electric heaters from their homes. They all sat together around the egg and sang Christmas carols all day long, trying to encourage the egg-wobbler to wobble its way out!

After a little while, Snozzletrump inspected the egg, running his hands over every inch of its shell. When he had finished, he turned to face the waiting crowd with a sorrowful expression on his sweaty face.

'The egg that sits behind my back has not one single hatching crack.'

Santa let out a long sigh. He knew the time had come for him to step down from the egg and get ready for . . .

A great noise echoed around the room. All the elves jumped to their feet excitedly.

'Shush, everyone!' hissed Santa. From on top of the egg he put his hand down and felt the smooth shell. He ran his hand along the shiny surface, which was no longer cold and frozen but actually quite warm. Suddenly he stopped moving his hand. He'd felt something. He moved his fingers back a few millimetres, and there it was: a very thin but very definite crack in the eggshell!

'It's hatching time!' Santa bellowed.

A hushed excitement spread like magic throughout the room as Santa carefully climbed down from the egg and stood with all his elves, watching.

Then, out of nowhere, a very deep rumble could be heard. It was a most peculiar sound, almost like the rumble of a distant train, or like a very loud, very hungry tummy. The rumble was coming from *inside* the egg! Santa looked at the eight elves who had found the egg, who were all looking excitedly nervous – or maybe they were nervously excited. It was hard to tell.

The rumble grew louder. The egg started to wobble. Suddenly that tiny crack broke open a little more. Now

there was a *big, deep, dark* crack, which you could almost
see into.

All the elves held hands very tightly. Snozzletrump let
out a nervous snozzletrump.

Then, just as suddenly as it had all started, everything
seemed to stop.

The rumble stopped.

The wobbling stopped.

There were no more cracks appearing.

Just silence.

Everyone in the room was still, except for Santa. He
took one brave step forward and peered into the shell.
He couldn't see much. It was all very dark – but it looked
like there was something shiny inside. As Santa leant in
for a closer look, that shiny something BLINKED!

'It's an EYE!' gasped Santa.

And the eye was looking out at everyone in the room!

Santa almost jumped out of his skin, which made all
the elves almost jump out of their skins! Once they'd all
got back in their skins, everyone laughed nervously at
themselves for being such scaredycats.

That's when it happened.

CracKᵃBooooOOM!

Santa and the elves dived for cover as the egg exploded into a billion sparkly pieces, showering the room in shimmering shell that fell like glitter dust over their heads.

Slowly, Santa got to his feet and sneezed off some of the shell dust from his moustache and beard. He brushed glitter from his underpants and wiped his full-moon spectacles, and when he put them back on his nose he couldn't quite believe what his eyes saw. In the middle of the room, where the egg stood moments ago, was something impossible. But this was the North Pole where *anything* is possible.

'What is it?' cried the elves.

Then they heard a

RoooOOAAR!

Inside the Egg

'Well, bless my kringles,' Santa said with a tear in his eye. 'It's a baby **DINOSAUR!**'

CHAPTER 5

THE CHRISTMASAURUS

 great chitter-natter arose amongst the elves as they fired a relentless round of rhyming questions at Santa.

'What type of dinosaur?'
'What's its name?'
'Is it dangerous?'
'Or is it tame?'
'If it's a girl can we call her Ginny?'
'I think it's a boy! *Look*, he's got a thingy!'

'THAT'S ENOUGH!' Santa commanded, gesturing

for the giddy elves to settle down. He wanted to get a better look at the new, freshly hatched member of their North Pole family (who was indeed a boy dinosaur – thank you, Snozzletrump). Santa slowly walked over to this impossible creature sitting on the floor. The baby dinosaur was unlike any dinosaur Santa had ever seen in any book or museum.

At first glance, the dinosaur had deep blue scaly skin that was so reflective and shiny he could almost have been a magnificent, translucent ice sculpture. But as Santa stepped closer he saw that the dinosaur's skin was a combination of thousands of rich colours that made a strange pattern down his spine. Perhaps it was because the dinosaur had been frozen in the ice for so long, or maybe it was pure coincidence, but the pattern on his back looked as if a scattering of large, perfectly symmetrical snowflakes had fallen on his head and all the way down to the tip of his long tail, which was curled up around him like that of a giant, scaly cat.

The baby dinosaur blinked and Santa saw that he was nervous. He held out one of his big, warm hands and looked deep into the dinosaur's eyes, and the dinosaur relaxed instantly. That was one of Santa's special tricks: if you looked into Santa's kind, jolly eyes, all your troubles and worries would melt away like icicles in the sunshine.

Santa put his hand on the dinosaur's scaly head and said happily, 'You arrived just in time for me to say this to you – *Merry Christmas*!' And as he patted the dinosaur's head his tongue flopped merrily out of his

smiling mouth. After millions of years inside a frozen egg he couldn't have defrosted in a more magical place.

'Hmmmm, now what sort of dinosaur are you?' Santa said to himself whilst combing bits of eggshell from his beard. 'Snozzletrump! Skip to the library, please, and fetch the encyclopaedia.'

'Certainly, Your Merriness, I'll fetch it – *Argh* . . .' Snozzletrump moaned as Santa booted him out of the room before he could finish his rhyme. Moments later, the elf came skipping back in, carrying an enormously thick book on his head.

'Right!' Santa said, pushing up his brass-framed spectacles. Lifting the book from the elf, he began flicking through the pages. 'Let's see . . . apple pie . . . big bogies . . . bigger bogies . . . candyfloss . . . here we are! Dinosaurs!' Santa threw the book open on to the ground for all the elves to see.

On the pages were hundreds of illustrations of every kind of dinosaur you could possibly think of. Scaly ones with horns, horny ones with scales, red ones with claws, blue ones with paws, feathery ones with flappers, leathery ones with snappers, meat-eaty ones, veg-gobbly ones . . .

BUT not a single drawing or description of the hundreds and hundreds in the book looked anything like the dinosaur sitting in front of them.

The elves cried out, 'He's not in here! Honest, look! He's not any dinosaur in this book!'

Just then a great-grandfather clock chimed and Spudcheeks the elf came hurrying into the room singing with some urgency:

> 'The sleigh is loaded and ready to go;
> You must leave now with a ho, ho, ho.
> The reindeer are fed and fit to fly!
> I've polished your goggles to protect your eyes.
> The children are sleeping and waiting for toys –
> We'll look after this dinosaur, won't we, boys?'

'AND GIRLS!' shouted Starlump and Sparklefoot, even though it didn't rhyme.

The rest of the eight elves who had discovered the frozen egg all cheered in agreement. Spudcheeks was right. It was time for Santa to leave and to do his duty, for it was Christmas Eve, the one night of the year that

Santa could not be distracted. Santa nodded and stood up to go, but before he left the room he felt a tiny tap-tap on his leg. He looked down and saw Sprout the elf standing at his boot, staring up whilst nervously stroking the baby dinosaur's smooth scales.

'Santa, please don't leave before you name this Christmas dinosaur!' Sprout said ever so sweetly.

'Hmmmm, a Christmas dinosaur . . .' Santa said to himself.

A wide, merry smile suddenly grew on his face.

A *Christmas* dinosaur!

Santa cleared his throat, waved for silence and in his deepest, richest voice spoke these words:

> 'My wondrous little North Pole elves,
> You must congratulate yourselves,
> For I believe beyond a doubt
> A miracle has come about.
> It's sitting right here on the floor,
> Looking like no other dinosaur.'

All the elves listened with tears welling in their tiny elf

eyeballs. It wasn't often Santa spoke to them like this, but when he did, boy, did he do it with style!

He continued:

> 'Another year you've served me well,
> Through good times and the tough as well.
> But I shall not forget the night
> An egg was dug up from the ice.
> And here he sits, this nameless creature,
> With such fantastic festive features,
> That there is just one name for him –
> Come one, come all, come hear me sing . . .
> This Christmas dinosaur before us
> Shall henceforth be known as the
> Christmasaurus!'

The Christmasaurus let out a long happy roar and the North Pole elves replied with a cheer. They sang and danced a merry celebration with their new dinosaur friend long into the night, while Santa delivered presents all around the world. It was a Christmas Eve that none of them would ever forget.

Chapter Six

MAGNIFICENTLY MAGICAL FLYING REINDEER

For the Christmasaurus, growing up in the North Pole was awesomely fun. He would watch the polar bears play ping-pong. He'd watch the forest fairies fish for fidgets – little swimming insects that fairies eat as snacks (they taste like Marmite). He'd watch the snowmen ice skate and the walruses waltz.

But, of course, he spent most of his time with Santa and the eight elves who'd found him: Snozzletrump,

Specklehump, Sparklefoot, Sugarsnout, Starlump, Spudcheeks, Snowcrumb and Sprout. They were like family to the Christmasaurus.

As the Christmasaurus grew, they looked after him, fed him his daily serving of forty-two mince pies, washed him with the happy tears of fairies (fairy liquid), walked him three times an hour and did pretty much everything that your mum and dad do for you. Those eight little elves, as well as Santa himself, were the closest thing to parents that the Christmasaurus had and he loved them all very much indeed.

But even though Santa and the elves were a wonderful family, the Christmasaurus was sometimes very, very lonely.

He felt lonely because he was different.

He was the *only* dinosaur in the world. There were lots of elves, lots of polar bears, lots of walruses and whales and snowmen and forest fairies . . . but there was only *one* of him, and that made him rather sad.

Whenever the Christmasaurus felt sad he knew there was only one thing that would cheer him up. He would go and visit his favourite of all the creatures in the North Pole: Santa's Magnificently Magical *Flying* Reindeer!

Santa's Magnificently Magical Flying Reindeer were the most wondrous creatures you could possibly imagine. Clear your head for a moment and I'll help you picture one.

Imagine a pair of soft, velvety antlers. Now double their softness.

Imagine a pair of deep, twinkling black eyes. Like a starry sky.

Imagine a dark brown fur coat speckled with jingly-jangly bells.

Imagine four bright golden hooves that seem to glow from within.

Now imagine this creature flying around ten metres above your head and – *voila!* There you have one of Santa's Magnificently Magical Flying Reindeer.

The Christmasaurus thought they were magnificent too. He would spend hour after hour just watching them fly about in circles, high over his head. You see, the Christmasaurus had a secret . . .

He wished that he could fly up there with them.

The Christmasaurus thought that if only he could fly like a reindeer then maybe he wouldn't be so different. Perhaps one day he might even be allowed to pull Santa's sleigh!

Well, once that idea had found its way into the Christmasaurus's head, there wasn't a fidget's chance in the North Pole of getting it out! Pulling Santa's sleigh on Christmas Eve with the

Magnificently Magical Flying Reindeer became the Christmasaurus's life ambition, and from that moment on it was all he ever thought about.

If a reindeer can fly, then so can I! he would think to himself in his dinosaur thoughts. He promised himself that he would do whatever it took to get his scaly dinosaur tail off the ground and into the air with the reindeer.

So, the Christmasaurus started eating the same food as the reindeer and drinking the same drinks as the reindeer. He even started sleeping in the stables with the reindeer in the hope that whatever magic made them fly might rub off on him.

But, you see, it wasn't as simple as that. There was a special reason why the reindeer could fly, and it wasn't in their food or their drink. It wasn't the way they slept, and it wasn't to do with their great velvety antlers or glowing golden hooves. There was a *deeper* magic at work, and it was the strongest, oldest kind of magic that exists.

All around the world there are millions of children, just like you, who all know about Santa's flying reindeer.

They don't just *think* Santa's reindeer can fly. Those millions of children *believe* that Santa's reindeer can fly. They believe beyond any shadow of doubt, and *belief* is the most powerful magic there is. Believing is the only magic that makes the utterly impossible completely possible, and the undoubtedly undoable undeniably doable! And of all the different kinds of belief there are the belief of a child is by far the most unbelievably unstoppable.

If all the children in the world suddenly stopped believing in Santa and flying reindeer and all the wonderful things in the North Pole, then all of those fantastic things would pop out of existence like the bursting of a bubble! That's why believing is so important. It's what keeps magic alive.

And so you can see the problem. Not one child on Planet Earth knew that there was a dinosaur living in the North Pole. Not one child *believed* that a dinosaur *could* fly. So it was hopeless. No matter how fast the Christmasaurus ran, no matter how high the Christmasaurus jumped, without the belief of a child he just couldn't fly.

MAGNIFICENTLY MAGICAL FLYING REINDEER

*

On the first of December, the Christmasaurus was walking alone around the outskirts of the elf city with his head hanging low. The North Pole was getting into the full swing of Christmas, and the Christmasaurus saw a great snowman snowball fight in the distant snowfields – but he was terrible at throwing snowballs with his tiny little dinosaur arms. The elves had erected the most enormous Christmas tree in the centre of the ranch but he was completely rubbish at decorating Christmas trees, the tinsel always got caught up in his claws and tail. He couldn't swim like the narwhals, or wrap presents like the fairies. In fact, when he thought about it, the Christmasaurus realized just how different he was. He really didn't fit in at all!

The Christmasaurus let out a very low, very sad roar, leaving long, lonely clawprints behind him, his scaly tail dragging in the snow. He stared out into the distance over the great North Pole mountains, and as the Northern Lights splashed their greens and blues across the sky he wondered if there was anybody else in the whole wide world who was like him. Was there

anybody out there who knew what it was like to be different?

What the Christmasaurus didn't know was that there *was* someone, a long way away, who was looking up at the sky just like him, wondering the exact same thing. Someone who knew just what it was like to be different.

You've already met him, of course.

That someone was a small boy called William Trundle.

CHAPTER SEVEN

THE THING ABOUT WILLIAM

Three Christmases had passed since we first met William – and this ten-year-old version of him wasn't quite the chirpy fella he used to be.

But before we get into that there's something else you should know about him. You see, the thing about William was that William couldn't walk. William has a wheelchair.

Did I forget to mention that? Sorry!

William had been in a nasty, horrible accident when he was a little boy and that was the sad day he had

lost his mother and gained a wheelchair. It had been awful and difficult, but it was a long time ago.

Other than his shiny, red, dino-decorated wheelchair, he was just like every other kid now. He went to school like every other kid, liked watching TV like every other kid, forgot his homework like every other kid, and occasionally picked his nose and ate it like every other kid. (We've all done it!)

All the other kids at Holly Heath Primary School had got so used to William having a wheelchair that they didn't even notice it any more.

That was until *she* started.

The new girl who had moved into a house across the

street from William, and had joined William's class last year.

She changed everything.

Her name was Brenda Payne.

Brenda was the meanest girl in the whole school, possibly the world. She was a greedy, loud, bossy bully who always had to be the centre of attention. She had annoyingly perfect twirly blonde hair (twirls are like curls that are showing off) and horribly straight, 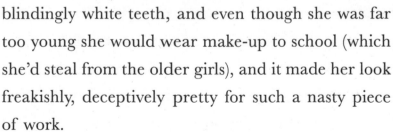 blindingly white teeth, and even though she was far too young she would wear make-up to school (which she'd steal from the older girls), and it made her look freakishly, deceptively pretty for such a nasty piece of work.

Brenda's first day at school had started out just fine.

She gave William that awkward, sad look that most people gave him when they first saw his wheelchair, but William was used to *that* look. He'd had years of experience of *that* look, so he just did what he always did: he smiled. William had such a brilliant, confident smile that it shone out, just like that really strong torch you have lying in your cupboard at home that you never use. His smile instantly made *that* look vanish from Brenda's face.

It was at lunchtime that it all went horribly wrong.

The whole school was waiting impatiently in line for school dinner, which usually comprised something that sort of looked like chicken, coated in something that sort of looked like breadcrumbs, accompanied by soggy strips of potato that they called chips, and a compulsory scoop of some sort of green mush.

The school cafeteria was a large, open space with a serving station along one wall and dozens of tables and chairs lined up across the permanently sticky floor. Although lunchtime was monitored by Old Man Wrinkleface – the school caretaker – he could usually be found snoozing in the corner with his feet on an upturned bucket, his hand clasping a flask of lukewarm tea and his hearing aid switched off.

Lunchtime belonged to the kids!

This was every new kid's nightmare.

The stares.

The glares.

The flares. (Old Man Wrinkleface always wore them.)

The air was thick with judgement, so the last person you would want to be on that day was Brenda Payne. She was first in line to get served, followed closely by William, who watched as Brenda nervously handed over her tray for the dinner ladies to slop the sludge on to her plastic plate. William followed suit and got his dinner, but as he spun his wheelchair round towards the cutlery table he felt a bump under one of his wheels and heard an awful sound.

'OUCH! THAT'S MY FOOT!' screamed Brenda
at the top of her squeakily perfect voice. She jumped
backwards in pain, sending her tray of barely edible
sludge flying up into the air.

For a second everything seemed to float over Brenda's
head: the chicken, the green slop, the soggy potato. It
all hung there, just long enough for Brenda to look deep
into William's eyes, and it was at that very moment that
he knew he'd just made an enemy.

CRASH! SPLAT! SPLOSH!

Brenda, the new girl, was standing in the middle of the cafeteria covered in her school dinner, surrounded by the entire school.

The sound of laughter erupted like a volcano. Children pointed and howled with glee, the cafeteria lit up with the flashes of hundreds of camera phones. #NewGirlGetsSplattered was trending worldwide within seconds. Even Gregory Guff, the little kid who peed his pants every lunchtime, was peeing his pants laughing at Brenda!

But what Brenda did next took everyone by surprise.

She didn't cry.

She didn't make a dash for the exit.

Brenda stood very still, very silent, and didn't take her eyes off William.

'I'm so, so sorry! It was an accident. I didn't see you behind me,' William apologized, but it was hard to make his voice heard over the laughter.

Brenda still said nothing. She just waited. Then, as the laughter started to quieten down, she slowly raised her left hand and removed the plastic plate that was sitting upside down on her head. Then she scooped up a huge handful of the compulsory green slop from her face and piled it high on to the plate.

She raised her hand in the air like she was

74

conducting an orchestra and the strangest silence fell over the cafeteria. It was the quietest William had ever heard it.

'My name is Brenda Payne,' she announced to the school as some wobbly chicken slipped from her shoulder on to the floor.

Nobody laughed.

'I am the new girl.'

And with those words, she pulled back her hand and launched the plate of green slop into William's face at point-blank range!

It hit him with such a wallop that it sent his wheelchair whizzing backwards across the cafeteria, through the emergency exit, and out into the car park. He came to a stop in a parking space reserved for teachers. As if that wasn't bad enough, a traffic warden then appeared out of nowhere and gave him a ticket for not parking his wheelchair in a disabled bay.

'Anyone have any questions?' Brenda asked the school, but by this point everyone was too scared to even make eye contact with her. She picked up her tray, marched over to the serving station and scooped herself some fresh sludge, then sat down at the head of the central table and began to eat her lunch.

From that moment on, Brenda Payne ran the school.

CHAPTER EIGHT

WHEELY WILLIAM

Life for William changed after that day.

It happened slowly at first, just little things. He'd notice that some of his friends stopped offering to wheel him up the ramp into school in the mornings, and no one would help him pick up his pencil when it dropped on the floor and rolled out of reach. Then, as the weeks went by, no one would sit with him at lunchtime. Whatever table he'd wheel himself to would quickly empty, and he'd have to eat his sloppy school dinner alone. And so he found that he had become what is commonly known as a loner. Billy-no-mates. The weirdo with the wheels. And it was all down to Brenda.

As I'm sure you can imagine, this made William very sad. He used to be so popular, but now all the other *normal* kids in his school, with *normal* legs, would call him names like '*Wheely* William' or '*Wheeliam*'. One particularly nasty person – Brenda Payne, of course – went that one step further, and made up a little song that went like this:

Wheely William can't walk around!
Wheely William just rolls along the ground!
He can't kick a ball!
He can't run fast!
He can't play with us
Just rolls on past.

Wheely William goes whizzing down the street!
Wheely William has rocks for feet!
He can't climb trees!
He doesn't walk!
Wheel away, William –
We don't want to talk!

WHEELY WILLIAM

Wheely William sitting in a chair;
Wheely William rolls everywhere!
He can't do jumps!
He can't even stand!
To go upstairs
He uses a ramp!

It wasn't long before Brenda's nastiness had infected the whole school, like a disease that turned everyone into William-hating zombies! She'd bullied herself an army of William-haters. The children who used to be his friends now treated him like he wasn't one of *them* any more. Like he didn't belong there. Like he was smelly or something.

The thing about Brenda was that she wasn't like most bullies. Most bullies are stupid, jealous jellybrains, but not Brenda Payne. Brenda was as smart as she was pretty, and she used both of those things to get whatever she wanted. She wasn't the strongest kid in the playground – in fact, there were plenty of children who could have easily knocked her perfect teeth out if they'd wanted to – but Brenda had a way of making those kids *not* want to! She didn't need to punch kids or steal things (although she did both of those things regularly) because, if she wanted, she could bully you with just a look. She only needed to glance at William and it sent shivers running right through him, which made him feel completely and utterly pathetic.

Since the day William had accidentally rolled over her foot, it was as if making his life hell had become Brenda's only purpose in life.

She would sneak up behind him during class and stick pins in his wheelchair tyres so that they went flat.

As winter settled in, she started coming to school an hour early to pour water on the wheelchair ramp, so that by the time William arrived it was covered in solid ice and he couldn't get up it at all, meaning the teachers had to lift him up the stairs.

Completely humiliating!

But Brenda Payne's speciality was her throw.

Of course, William had known exactly how face-smashingly accurate Brenda's throw was since her first day at school, when she'd launched the handful of horrible slop at his head. She had an expert aim and

could hit her target from an impressive distance. She'd
use her skill to hurl sticks like javelins from the far side
of the playground straight into the spokes of William's
wheels. They'd jam the wheels so suddenly that
his wheelchair would stop . . . but William
wouldn't. He'd carry on going, bouncing
along the ground on his bottom to
the sound of laughter from *Brenda
Payne's Army of Pain* – that's the
name William gave them:
his old friends!

After that happened five times, William had a seatbelt fitted to his wheelchair so at least he wouldn't fall out.

Before, William used to happily slip out of bed into his wheelchair and whizz off to school, but those days were gone. Now he would wake up, look at his chair, sigh a deeply miserable sigh, and think to himself, *What rotten thing is she going to do today?*

But of all the rotten things Brenda did to William, the worst of all was about to come one snowy Friday afternoon at the beginning of December – the very day the Christmasaurus was feeling glum far away in the North Pole, in fact.

She didn't use sticks or pins. She used the most powerful weapon of all.

Words.

Their teacher, Mrs Dribblepot, had just popped out to the loo, and as Brenda never missed an opportunity to make William's life miserable, as soon as the door clicked shut, a shiny black stapler flew across the classroom, straight at William's head! William tried to block it with his exercise book, but the force of the throw was so strong that the book smacked him straight in the face and the stapler stapled it to his forehead!

The noise that followed sounded like a laughter bomb exploding in the classroom.

That's when William felt it happening.

He couldn't stop it.

The worst thing possible.

He began to cry!

'Are you crying?' asked Brenda with a huge, evil smile expanding across her pretty face.

'No!' lied William, quickly wiping the tears from his cheeks and plucking the staple out of his forehead.

'You are, aren't you! Wheely's crying, everyone! Look!' Brenda called out, and the laughter level doubled. It wasn't that anyone actually found it funny. It was because they were scared not to laugh!

'Crybaby, crybaby!' Brenda chanted. 'Why don't you go crying to your mummy?'

The whole room suddenly fell silent.

Whispers of '*Brenda doesn't know!*' quickly circled the classroom.

'Know what?' Brenda demanded.

'He doesn't have a mum,' called out Freddie, the tallest kid in the class, from the back of the room.

'You don't have a mum?' asked Brenda.

'He lives with his dad,' yelled Lola, one of William's pre-Brenda friends.

Brenda paused for a moment, then that smile grew back.

'Well, it's your dad I feel sorry for,' she said, casually twiddling a pencil around in her perfectly twirly hair. 'I mean, can you imagine having to live with Wheely William? It's hard enough going to school with him! It must be so difficult for your poor old daddy, pushing you around everywhere on his own. You must feel like such a lump of uselessness. I know *I* would if *I* were like you . . . Thank goodness I'm not!'

William bit his lip hard, trying to stop himself from shouting something horrible back at her. He knew only tears would come out if he tried.

'And I'm not surprised your dad looks so lonely all the time. He's the loony one who wears those awful Christmas jumpers all year round, right? I bet he still believes in Santa, like a little baby! I mean, who on earth would ever marry *him*? Christmas jumpers AND Wheely William. Who would ever want to be *your* mum!'

With those final, awful words, she stretched her legs out and gave a pretend yawn.

The stunned silence was only broken by Mrs Dribblepot returning from the loo.

That afternoon, when the school bell rang and it was time to go home, William couldn't help hearing Brenda's words over and over again and again in his head. He looked out through the front gates of the school and saw mums and dads waiting happily as their children skipped across the playground towards them.

Then he saw his dad.

His tired-looking dad.

Mr Trundle was standing alone to one side of the

school gate, wearing his favourite Christmas jumper (he'd knitted it himself) while all the other parents were nattering away in a big group. As William wheeled closer, he heard them say things like:

'Great pot roast the other night, Jacqui!'

'Looking forward to the Christmas party, Pete.'

'I'll see you for that run tomorrow morning, Jenny.'

William looked from one happy family to another and a strange feeling swirled around in his stomach, like water going down a plughole. The feeling was emptiness. He'd never noticed it before, but now that he felt it he was almost certain it had always been there.

'Hello, son!' Mr Trundle said with a smile.

But William was so full of this newfound emptiness that he just wheeled past Mr Trundle and didn't say a word.

Was Brenda right? Was Mr Trundle really lonely?

Why wasn't he friends with any of the other parents? William couldn't remember the last time Mr Trundle had gone to a party or out for a walk or had even had a cup of coffee with anyone.

Why had he never married again, after William's

mother had died? Lots of kids in William's class had stepmothers and stepfathers.

Was it all because William was the way he was? Would anyone ever want to be a mother to a boy like him?

William had never felt so different. So lonely. So guilty.

Brenda had planted those awful words like rotten seeds in William's brain, and they were beginning to grow into rotten thoughts . . . thoughts that Brenda was about to spectacularly interrupt.

CHAPTER NINE

BRENDA THE REVENGER

O n the way home that same snowy Friday afternoon, Mr Trundle had to pop into the supermarket. William wheeled himself straight to his favourite aisle: the breakfast cereal aisle. He could spend hours there, choosing which box to take home. Chocolate-covered frosty ones or frosty-covered chocolate ones were his favourites, although his dad usually made him get something with less frosty chocolate stuff and more fruity-grain stuff. William thought those ones tasted like bird food!

On this particular day, William had just wheeled himself to the end of the cereal aisle for the seventh

time, lost in feelings of emptiness and worries about his lonely dad, when he heard giggling behind him.

He spun his wheelchair round and stared down the long aisle of breakfast munch, but there was no one there.

How odd.

Suddenly, some scurrying footsteps rushed past, but by the time he'd whizzed his chair round, whoever it was had gone.

'Hello?' William called, but no one answered.

He was just about to go to find his dad when he saw something rather strange out of the corner of his eye. Something white and floaty was coming towards him from the far end of the cereal aisle at great speed. He couldn't quite make out what it was. He'd never seen anything like it before. It was large and white and floating through the air, continuously changing shape, wibbling and blobbling like a thick, wet ghost!

William froze in his wheelchair. He didn't know what to do. He felt completely helpless as this weird blob of whiteness flew through the air towards him, until . . .

William was hit square in the face by a flying super-sized tub of double-thick, extra-creamy pouring cream!

You wouldn't believe how much cream there was! However much you're imagining, double it . . . then add a bit more, and that's still probably not quite enough.

William was coated from head to toe. He looked like a delicious ghost!

But that wasn't all. The flying wave of dairy hit him with such force that it sent his wheelchair whooshing backwards, slipping and sliding on the cream-covered floor of the cereal aisle, until he smashed into the shelves. Luckily the cardboard boxes of his favourite frosted choco-drops crumpled behind him, softening the impact – but as one box fell over it knocked another box, which knocked over the next box, and the one after that . . . until suddenly every box was knocking over every box next to it, like a crazy game of breakfast-cereal dominoes!

The boxes fell one after the other. There was an almighty crash as clouds of flakes and puffs of corn and oats filled the air. Shoppers ran for the fire escapes in a frosted flake frenzy, the likes of which had never been seen before – and right in the middle of the commotion was William, covered from head to toe in double-thick, extra-creamy pouring cream, sprinkled with every sort of breakfast cereal you could possibly imagine.

Then, just as William thought it was over, the unusual amount of wholegrain dust in the air set off the fire sprinklers, and the aisles were flooded with freezing water. The water mixed with the double-thick, extra-creamy cream, transforming the supermarket into

the world's largest bowl of cereal. Within ten minutes officials from Guinness World Records showed up, confirmed it and hung a plaque on the wall!

William knew there was only one person mean enough to throw cream at someone in a supermarket while they are choosing their cereal. At that moment, the water from the sprinklers showered away some of the thick dairy from his eyes, just in time for him to see the long golden twirls of Brenda Payne as she skipped merrily away and made her escape through the fire exit.

Mr Trundle wheeled his sad, soggy son home through the crowded, snow-covered streets. Mums and dads wandered merrily with their children through the falling snowflakes with that twinkle of Christmas magic in their eyes, but William couldn't help feeling absolutely rotten.

Feeling rotten is much worse than feeling just bad or sad. Feeling rotten is when it seems like no one else in the world understands how you're feeling. When you're feeling rotten, everything seems rotten around you. For example, can you think of the tastiest, scrummiest, yummiest, cheesiest cheeseburger you've ever had? Well, even if William had eaten that exact same cheeseburger right then, it would have tasted absolutely rotten to him. That's how rottenly rotten he was feeling!

Brenda the Revenger

Everyone feels rotten from time to time, and that's perfectly OK – but no little boy or girl should feel rotten at Christmastime. That's just rotten!

Right then, William didn't care about Christmas. In fact, at that moment, he didn't feel like caring much about anything at all. William just wanted to go to his rotten home and go to rotten bed.

With their heads full of worries, Mr Trundle and William trundled home, unaware that somewhere close behind them, hiding in the shadows, someone was watching them.

William was being followed!

CHAPTER TEN

WHAT WILLIAM WANTS

That evening, William sat in his wheelchair at the dinner table in his wonky little home. Mr Trundle had made him his favourite meal (golden crumby fishy fingers and crispy-crunch potato waffles with baked beans), but to William it just looked like rotten plateful of rottenness.

'I'm not hungry, Dad,' William said. 'Can I go to bed early, please?'

Mr Trundle looked at William with that look that parents have when they're worried but trying not to look worried.

WHAT WILLIAM WANTS

'Of course you can, my Willypoos,' said Mr Trundle, trying to make William smile.

'I hate it when you call me that, Dad. Why can't we just be like a normal family!' William snapped, and wheeled himself away from the *rotten* dinner table, out of the *stinking* dining room, down the *crummy* hallway and into his *rubbish* bedroom, which was on the ground floor next to the living room.

He parked his chair right next to his bed and pulled himself out so that he was sitting on top of his dinosaur-patterned bed covers. He wriggled out of his clothes and put on his favourite pair of pyjamas (which were also dinosaur-patterned), and slid his favourite bedtime story out from under his pillow (which was a very silly story about a dinosaur that pooped a planet). Since the day Brenda Payne had entered his life and made being in a wheelchair completely rotten, dinosaurs had been just about the only thing that could cheer William up.

Just then, Mr Trundle appeared in William's doorway carrying a packet of William's favourite chocolate-chip cookies and a large mug of warm milk. William's rotten levels dropped dramatically when he saw them.

A few minutes later, they'd finished reading William's favourite silly book, the packet of biscuits was empty, and they were just starting to share the warm mug of milk when Mr Trundle said, 'Have you thought about what you're going to ask Santa for this year, William?'

William wiped the milky moustache away from his lips and suddenly felt a little bit rotten again.

'My dear boy, what on earth is wrong?' Mr Trundle asked.

'Well . . . it's . . . it's just that . . . I don't think Santa can get me what I want this year, Dad,' William said sadly.

Of course, Mr Trundle had heard him say that before, but this year William wasn't staring longingly at his dinosaur posters. The emptiness in his stomach was telling him he wanted something far greater than that.

William looked up at his dad, who was sitting on the edge of his bed, and then his eyes were caught by the empty air sitting next to Mr Trundle. He finally looked down at his legs and sighed a deeply unhappy sigh. For the first time in his life, he was beginning to wish he wasn't the way he was. As though all the problems in the world came back around to one thing: his legs.

Mr Trundle tucked William into bed and pulled out a pen and William's favourite dinosaur notebook from the desk in the corner of the room.

'Well, perhaps you're asking Santa for the wrong thing,' Mr Trundle said. 'Before you go to sleep, I want you to have a think about what you *really* want this year and write your letter to Santa.'

William still felt a little troubled. There was something he wanted to say, but didn't quite know how to say it. Still, he knew that sometimes the hardest things to say are the most important ones. So he took a breath and said, 'Dad . . .'

'Yes, William?' replied Mr Trundle, as he searched the packet of biscuits for any remaining crumbs.

'Are you . . . lonely?' asked William.

Mr Trundle paused in amazement.

'My dear Willypoos . . . I mean, *William*. What on earth made you think that?' he said, a tiny wobble in his voice.

99

'It's just that – well – I've been thinking it because . . . you spend all of your time looking after me, because I am the way I am.'

'And that's just the way I like it,' said Mr Trundle sharply.

'But are you happy?' asked William. 'Like, *really* happy?'

'Happier than a bauble on a Christmas tree. Now I won't hear any more of this nonsense.'

They both sat quietly for a moment. William looked around his bedroom at the photos hanging on the wall and sitting on the shelf. They were all of just two people. Him and his dad.

'Now, there's time for one more story before bed. What would you like?' Mr Trundle asked.

'The story you used to tell me, about the elves and Santa and the North Pole!' William said. His dad told that one the best.

But as Mr Trundle started talking William's mind started wandering and wondering. Something that Brenda had said that day was stuck in his mind. *I bet he still believes in Santa!*

WHAT WILLIAM WANTS

'What's on your mind, son?' asked Mr Trundle.

'Dad. This story. Is it . . . true? Is it real or just make-believe?' asked William, almost as if he were scared to hear the answer.

Mr Trundle peered down at William through the round spectacles perched on his nose (which were always dirty), and smiled softly, as though he'd been expecting William to ask this exact question.

'Now, William, *that* is a very good question,' said Mr Trundle as he made himself comfortable on William's bed. He put his hand over his heart as he did whenever he was telling the truth.

'I *believe* this story is true. Therefore, it *is* true,' he said.

'But . . . how does that work?' questioned William, desperate to know more. 'If I've never seen something, how do I know it's real?'

'Ah, William! You've got it the wrong way round!' said Mr Trundle, smiling. 'Believing has to come first. People who don't believe in things will never see those things. Believing is seeing.'

But William still looked uncertain.

'But, Dad, some kids at school don't believe in Santa. What if *I* believe he's real and someone else doesn't? If we both believe different things, then we can't both be right, can we?' asked William.

Mr Trundle thought for a moment, then suddenly picked up the mug and downed half the warm, creamy milk inside. 'Mmmmm,' he said, wiping his mouth. 'Now, look inside this mug and what do you see?'

'Well, you've drunk half of it, so it's half empty now!' said William, looking a little miffed that his dad had just slurped up so much of his delicious drink.

'Are you sure?' asked Mr Trundle. 'Do you *believe* it's half empty?'

'Yes, of course I believe it's half empty. I can see that it is!' said William.

'Well, I don't believe that at all,' said Mr Trundle, leaving William looking rather puzzled. Had his dad gone completely barmy? The mug was quite clearly half empty. It was plain as day. William was sure of it.

'I believe something completely different,' Mr Trundle continued with a little smile. 'I believe this mug of milk is not half empty . . . I believe it is half full!'

William looked at the half empty mug of milk in front of him for a moment before realizing that his dad might actually be right too. Even though he and his dad believed different things, they were *both* right.

'You see, William, we both believe completely opposite things, but it doesn't mean that either of us is wrong. This mug is both half empty AND half full at the same time,' said Mr Trundle as William sat there with the expression of a young boy whose mind is in the process of being completely blown. 'People believe all sorts of wild, wacky, weird and wonderful things, but it doesn't mean that anyone is wrong or that anyone is right. What is important isn't what is wrong, right, real, fake, true or false. What matters is that whatever you *believe* makes you a happier, better person.'

William was listening closely. 'But, Dad, what if I believe in something that doesn't really exist? Aren't I believing in nothing?' he asked worriedly.

'Believing in nothing is better than not believing in anything at all. Belief, William, is what makes the impossible possible. The undoable doable. And, whatever you believe in, William, you will most definitely find! I believed in the milk and found it. You believed in the emptiness and found that. Neither of us was wrong, but one of us was happier!' Mr Trundle finished, and gave the half-empty, half-full mug of milk to William.

'Thanks, Dad,' said William, and he gulped down the rest of the gloriously warm milk. He placed the mug full of emptiness on his bedside table and picked up the pen, ready to write his letter to Santa. Then he paused.

'So, Dad . . . if I really, *really* believe it, will there be one last chocolate-chip cookie in that packet for me?' asked William with a cheeky grin, knowing full well that they'd eaten all the cookies.

Mr Trundle looked in the empty cookie packet and shook his head.

'Oh, William, I think it would take a bit more than belief to make that happen!'

He leant over, placed one hand on William's pillow and gave him a kiss goodnight. 'Get some sleep after you've finished that letter to Santa. You can take it to the postbox in the morning,' said Mr Trundle.

Just before he left William alone in his bedroom, he stopped at the door. 'William, if you want *me* to be happy, then ask Santa for something that will make *you* happy,' he said. 'Something you've always wanted. Goodnight.'

William sat thinking of something to ask Santa for. He thought and thought and thought. He thought so hard that it made his brain hurt a bit. As he looked around his room, his old dinosaur posters caught his eye. He stared at them, looking for inspiration, when suddenly his face started aching. He caught a glimpse of his reflection in his bedroom window and realized he was smiling! He hadn't seen that look on his face for quite some time. William knew exactly what he wanted from Santa. He started scribbling his letter, which looked like this:

Dear Santa,

For Christmas this year I would like a lot of things that you probably can't give me, but a dinosaur would make me very happy!

Merry Christmas,
William Trundle

What William Wants

William folded the letter in half, popped it on his bedside table and switched off his bedside light with the dinosaur lampshade. As he wriggled down under the covers and laid his head on his pillow, he felt something crumbly on his cheek. There, sitting on the pillow right next to his head, was one last chocolate-chip cookie.

William smiled and whispered, 'Thanks, Dad,' before gobbling it up and going to sleep.

CHAPTER ELEVEN
WATCHING WILLIAM

The next morning, William woke up feeling a lot less rotten than he had the night before. Now he was just looking forward to popping his letter to Santa in the postbox on the way to visit his favourite place in the world: *the museum*!

William had loved visiting the museum for as long as he could remember, not just because Mr Trundle worked there part-time at the gift shop, so William got free dinosaur stickers, but because to William it was the most magical place in the world.

It was the only place where William could escape from the world when he was feeling rotten and see huge models of dinosaurs and real dinosaur bones and skeletons. At the museum, William didn't care that his friends had all deserted him and signed up to Brenda Payne's Army of Pain. He actually quite liked being on his own. He could be as slow as he liked, and get lost in his own imaginary world full of dinosaurs, and that's exactly what he planned to do today.

Mr Trundle wheeled William out of their wonky little house, which was covered from wonky chimney to wonky flowerbeds in colourful Christmas lights. He locked up and they went down the ramp that led from the front door on to the pavement outside, then headed through the town, William holding on tight to the letter for Santa.

As they wheeled down the street towards the big red postbox, which was now wearing a white hat of snow, they passed a woman who William had seen a few times before. She was a very pretty lady and, when she walked by, Mr Trundle said, 'Merry Christmas!' and nodded in a silly old-fashioned sort of way, as though he were tipping an invisible top hat. But the lady said nothing back. In fact, she quickly crossed over to the other side of the street, shaking her head disapprovingly.

'What a Scroogey lady!' said William.

'Naughty List for sure,' said Mr Trundle as he patted his invisible top hat back on his head. They both laughed as they continued towards the postbox. Suddenly, William applied the brakes on his wheelchair.

'What's wrong, son?' said Mr Trundle as they slowed to a stop.

William had stopped because he'd seen something up ahead, something that made his heart sink: a glimpse of perfect, twirly blonde hair peeping out from behind the red postbox.

Brenda Payne!

'Maybe I should post my letter tomorrow,' William said nervously. The last thing he wanted right now was to see that stinker!

'What on earth for, William? We're here now,' said Mr Trundle. 'Let's just pop it in the postbox and head to the muscum.'

Mr Trundle pushed on William's chair and they carried on towards the postbox and Brenda. What was she doing hanging out next to the postbox anyway? She was pacing back and forth as if she were waiting for someone to show up.

Then William saw her pause and smile as a little boy approached the postbox with his mother. William recognized him from school: it was Gregory, the boy who peed himself daily.

As they got nearer, William could see that Brenda was up to no good. She had that *look at me, I'm so perfect* sort of look on her face, but it didn't fool William. He slowed down again so that he could see exactly what she was up to.

Brenda had positioned herself in front of the postbox when Gregory walked up to post a letter. As he was about to reach up and pop it in the slot, Brenda's voice stopped him.

'Good morning! That looks like a letter to Santa. Am I right? Why don't you allow me to post that for you so you can get on with your Christmas shopping?' she said in such a sickly sweet voice that it almost made William's ears puke.

'Oh, that's very sweet of you, my dear,' said the boy's mother, completely fooled by Brenda's act. 'Go on, Gregory dear, give the nice girl your letter and say thank you.'

'Thank you,' Gregory said uncertainly, as he handed over his letter then disappeared round the corner with his mother.

That's when William saw her do it. Once Gregory was out of sight, Brenda carefully and precisely tore open his letter. Then she pulled out her school pencil case, which she'd been hiding behind the wall. She quickly Tippexed over Gregory's address, blew on it . . . blew on it a bit more, until Gregory's address had disappeared. Then she started scribbling something on the boy's letter!

What an evil, horrible thing to do, thought William. His blood was boiling. If he could have, he would have jumped out of his chair and chased Brenda Payne down the street. *She's up to something. I can't let her get away with it!* he said to himself.

'Dad, I want to post my letter . . . erm . . . alone . . . by myself,' William said.

Mr Trundle looked at the pretty little girl at the postbox, then smiled to himself.

'OK, William, I get it,' said Mr Trundle with a smirk. 'Don't want Daddy cramping your style, eh?'

William rolled his eyes at how uncool his dad was sounding, then wheeled himself towards the postbox whilst Mr Trundle stayed back and pretended he wasn't with him.

'Oi!' William said quietly to Brenda, suddenly feeling more like his old self.

'Well, look who it is . . . Wheely William! Are you allowed out in the snow in that *thing*? Wouldn't want your wheels to go all rusty,' Brenda said with a sickly sweet smile.

'What did you write on Greg's letter?' William demanded.

'Oh, this?' Brenda said innocently. 'It's nothing really, only my BEST PLAN EVER!'

William stared at Brenda, who was calmly using her glue stick to reseal the envelope of Gregory's letter.

'You see, *Wheely*, last year I was a little disappointed at the lack of presents in my stocking on Christmas morning. You may be surprised to find – I know I was – that *I* am on the *Naughty List* apparently!'

William wasn't surprised at all.

'Well, this year I'm not taking any chances. Even

though I've been a good girl this year . . . at least *I* think so . . . But just in case Santa – if he's even real! – thinks differently, there are plenty of goody two-shoes in this town who'll most definitely be on the *Nice List*. So I came up with a plan.' Brenda did a merrily evil skip around William's wheelchair, like she was some sort of crazed ballerina dancing to music in her head. 'It's rather genius, really. If I simply put my address on the goody-goody *Nice Listers'* letters, then all their presents will go to *my* house instead of theirs!' she said matter-of-factly, as if it were completely acceptable. 'Brilliant, isn't it?

Why struggle all year to be good when I've got a whole town of kids to be good for me, leaving me free to do whatever I want!'

William had heard enough. His face had gone purple with anger, as if he were about to explode in his chair, when a jolly voice called merrily from halfway down the street behind him.

'Everything all right, Willy?'

It was William's dad!

Willy?

WILLY?!

His dad had actually just called him . . . **WILLY!**

In front of Brenda Payne!

William almost died right there on the spot. His dad's pet name hit him like a truck carrying twenty tons of fresh embarrassment, and William felt as if he were drowning in it.

Brenda looked like she was about to burst with delighted evilness.

'Did your dad just call you . . . *Willy*?' She giggled quietly.

'DAD!' William groaned.

'What? You're not at school now, Willypoos. Technically I'm not breaking my promise!' called Mr Trundle cheekily from his spot halfway down the street.

'*Willypoos?* Oh my goodness, oh my goodness, that's brilliant!' howled Brenda, with genuine evil tears of evil laughter in her evil eyes. 'How have I never thought of that! Just you wait until we get back to –'

'You can't get away with stealing people's Christmas presents,' interrupted Willypoos . . . I mean, William. He thought that maybe bringing her attention back to her plan might distract her from this *Willy* nonsense.

'Wanna bet?' snapped Brenda sharply.

'I . . . I'll . . . I'll tell on you . . .' began William, but even as he was saying the words he realized how awfully silly and immature they sounded.

'No you won't, *Willypoos* . . . not unless you want the whole, entire school to know your daddy's little secret name for his *special ickle boy*!'

William stared at her.

Brenda smiled back.

There was nothing he could do. She was going to get away with it. He quickly tucked his own letter to Santa up his sleeve, making sure there was no way bum-faced Brenda could get it.

'Well, I'd better be going. I've got my address on enough nice kids' letters in there now to give me a good stockingful . . . or two . . . or three!' said Brenda, slipping Gregory Pee-Pants's letter into the dark slot of the postbox. 'Have a nice day . . . Willypoos!'

As she skipped off down the street, she waved happily to Mr Trundle and called out, 'Merry Christmas!' before disappearing round the corner.

Mr Trundle quickly joined William at the postbox, rubbing his hands together to keep them warm.

'She seems nice and friendly,' said Mr Trundle. 'Is she your *friend*?'

'No! She's definitely NOT my friend,' snapped William, but something in the way Mr Trundle smiled knowingly to himself made William think he didn't believe him.

'Go on then, son, pop your letter in and let's be going!' said Mr Trundle, eager to get out of the cold air.

William pushed Brenda and her evil plan to the back

of his mind and tried to enjoy the moment of posting his letter to Santa. It was always an exciting thing to do. But something felt different this year, and – oddly enough – it wasn't anything to do with Brenda.

William suddenly had the strangest feeling that he was being watched.

All the tiny little hairs on his arms and the back of his neck stood on end, and even though he was wrapped up in lots of lovely warm layers he found himself feeling a bit shivery.

It was a most peculiar sensation.

'Aren't you going to post your letter, William?' said Mr Trundle. William put the cold shivery feeling to the back of his mind as Mr Trundle lifted him out of his chair and held him close to the shadowy letter-slot, which sat open like a hungry mouth, waiting to be fed.

William gently popped his letter inside, and from the soft sound it made he could tell that the postbox must be very full – probably with letters from all the other *Nice List* children in town that now bore Brenda Payne's address!

As William got comfortable back in his chair, there it was again, that feeling that someone was watching him. His eyes scanned the street around him.

'What's the matter, William?' asked Mr Trundle, trying to see what William was looking at. But William couldn't see anyone else around. He could see all the way up the street back to their house, but there was no one there. The street was completely deserted. He must have been imagining it.

'I felt like someone was watching me . . . but . . . it's gone now,' said William, and so they left the postbox and continued their walk to the museum. But perhaps William should have paid more attention to the tiny little hairs on his arms and the back of his neck, because *those* hairs never lie. When those tiny little hairs stand up on end and make you go all shivery and goose-pimply you can be sure of one thing . . . someone *is* watching you.

WATCHING WILLIAM

What William had failed to see when he popped his letter through the dark rectangular letter-slot were two old, pokey eyes looking back out at him from inside the postbox.

Someone was there.

Someone was hiding inside it.

Someone was definitely watching William!

CHAPTER TWELVE

A STUFFED DINOSAUR

'The post is here!
The post is here!
Get off your bottom
It's that time of year!
Wipe out the sleep,
Pop on your specs,
Give the nice ones a tick
And the rotters an X!'

'Thank you very much, Snozzletrump!' called Santa as he slipped his extra large bottom into his squishy letter-reading chair for another day of letter reading.

A Stuffed Dinosaur

Things were getting rather busy in the North Pole, and so they should – it was December, after all. Letters were flying in from around the world and the very old, very crooked Christmas tree was sprouting out magic bean pods left, right and centre, up and down, and every which way you can imagine. The farmer elves were sowing the snowfields daily and the mining elves had started their first round of digging for toys.

The consumption of half crumpets had doubled in the last week alone and was showing no sign of slowing, as you can see from this handy Crumpet Consumption Graph:

The Christmasaurus was spending most of his time watching the Magnificently Magical Flying Reindeer on their nightly practice flights around the North Pole airspace. He stared at them and daydreamed wonderful flying dreams in his small little dinosaur brain whilst the rest of the North Pole was busy preparing Christmas.

There was one thing, though, that was about to put a cracker in the works. That thing was a letter, and that letter was from William Trundle!

Santa opened the letter, which was on top of the towering pile that Snozzletrump had just plopped on his desk, and read it aloud as he always did. *'Dear Santa, for Christmas this year I would like a lot of things that you probably can't give me, but a* dinosaur *would make me very happy! Merry Christmas . . . William Trundle.'*

There was no response at all from the ancient old Christmas tree. Santa frowned and read the letter aloud a second time, and then a third. He scratched his beard and tried again. But no matter how many times he read the letter the old Christmas tree never sprouted any bean pods at all! Maybe it was because the letter was so vague?

A Stuffed Dinosaur

'What sort of dinosaur does this young William Trundle want? A real one? Impossible! No child would ask for that. A *toy* dinosaur, then? A *stuffed* dinosaur? A *remote control robo*-dinosaur? The possibilities are endless! What do you make of this, Snozzletrump?' asked Santa as he took a sip from a cup of warm melted candy-cane juice.

Snozzletrump had heard Santa read the letter over and over again.

'It sounds like this kid's down in the dumps. That's the opinion of Snozzletrump.'

Santa screwed his face up at such an awful piece of elf poetry, which was definitely not up to Snozzletrump's usual standard. He sighed, held the letter in his large, flubby hands and took in a deep, calming breath through his white beard. His sky-coloured eyes closed and rolled back in his head, and after a few seconds he knew everything there was to know about William Trundle. This was another one of Santa's special powers.

Suddenly, his brain was full of William's life. He now knew about William's family, about William's accident when he was little, his wheelchair, his love of dinosaurs, and just how rotten life had been lately.

'Oh dear, this is a tough one,' said Santa. 'This boy needs something *really* special this year.'

At that moment Santa stood up, and in one massive swoosh of his jolly-fat arms he cleared everything away from the giant, messy workstation in his room.

'Sprout! Spudcheeks!' he called, and the two elves seemed to pop into existence from out of nowhere, right at Santa's side, their mouths full of buttery crumpet halves.

'What took you so long? Fetch me my tools, please. I'm going to make this one myself,' said Santa very seriously.

The look on the elves' faces was one of disbelief and pure delight.

A Stuffed Dinosaur

'HOORAY!' they cried in harmony. It wasn't very often that Santa handmade a present for someone. It happened only very occasionally, or in exceptional circumstances – but, when he did, those presents were always far more beautiful and special than any present that the elves dug up from the ice.

He once made a rocking horse for the Queen of England when she was a little girl, which he enchanted so that it came to life every Thursday night.

Another Christmas, he handmade a toy racing car for the Prince of Peru, who was a very naughty prince – almost on the Naughty List every year, but, instead of putting him on the Naughty List and forgetting about him, Santa enchanted the racing car so that it got smaller and smaller each time the young prince misbehaved! If he didn't stop being so naughty, it would eventually disappear completely, and so the naughty prince stopped being naughty! Santa was very clever like that.

The two elves sprinted out of the room and a few seconds later reappeared at Santa's doorway carrying a huge tool chest on their backs. It was overflowing with springs and cogs, bibs and bots, thingumabobs and all sorts of gadgets that only Santa knew how to use.

'Now go and tell the Christmasaurus that I need him at once, please! Hop to it, elves – we don't have all day!' said Santa, eager to get started.

> 'Yes, sir, right away –
> We're heading out the door!
> We haven't got all day
> To fetch that festive dinosaur!'

chirped the elves as they danced out of the room to fetch the Christmasaurus.

Moments later, they came riding in on the back of the Christmasaurus (the elves loved to ride on the Christmasaurus's back!), whose tongue was flapping happily out of his mouth, eager to find out why Santa needed him so urgently.

'My dear Christmasaurus, we have a job to do, and we have to do it right!' Santa said importantly. 'I need you to stand here for me and be very still, because I am going to make a toy dinosaur and I'm going to make it look like *you*!'

A Stuffed Dinosaur

The Christmasaurus's eyes widened in wonder at the thought of seeing Santa make a dinosaur! He'd never seen Santa make anything before. He climbed on to one of Santa's worktops, put his big dinosaur chin in the air, straightened his back and extended his long snowflake-patterned tail, trying to look like the perfect dinosaur model.

'First I'll need my extra-magnifying, super-zoom, au-toy-magic ogle-goggles!' Santa said as he strapped some brass goggles on to his head. The watching elves giggled as the goggles made Santa's eyes look like two giant baubles.

'Gloves!' he cried. Sprout and Spudcheeks quickly slipped two heavy leather gloves on to Santa's hands, and he started sifting through his tool chest. He had every toy-making contraption that had ever existed, and a few that didn't exist too! Long stuffing sticks for stuffing things, bendywendy things for bendywending things, flappyhappy things for making happyflappy things. You name it, Santa had it . . . and if you can't name it he probably had that too.

And so, as the December snow fell heavily at the

windows, Santa got to work. It wasn't easy. In fact, it was the hardest thing Santa had ever made. He worked all through the night until Starlump and Specklehump brought him breakfast – pancakes with a side of waffles, Santa's favourite – then he carried on working some more.

A Stuffed Dinosaur

All the elves crowded round to watch the master at work as the Christmasaurus sat as still as a statue in the warm glow from the fire. Santa chiselled and sawed, chopped and sewed, and didn't take any breaks. He only managed to stay awake by repeatedly drinking venti-sized coffees from the North Star-bucks coffee shop (with extra toffee-nut syrup and a splash of fresh reindeer milk).

Finally, Santa unstrapped the thick goggles from his head, which left big dark rings round his eyes.

'I think we're finished,' he said with a warm, proud smile, and he turned his creation round so that the Christmasaurus and all the elves could get a better look.

The crowd of elves gasped (in beautiful harmony) as they saw the finished toy dinosaur. They thought it was the most amazingly beautiful toy Santa had ever made. And it was. It really was.

The Christmasaurus shook out the pins and needles from his legs and hobbled over until he was face to face with Santa's masterpiece. He was nose to nose with the most perfectly detailed toy he had ever set eyes upon. It had soft, leathery skin with incredibly detailed stitching in Santa's own red cotton thread. He'd used two large golden buttons for its eyes, and for its stuffing Santa had cut a hole in his own quilted flying coat and poured in half of the wonderfully fluffy, double-duck feathers. (Double-duck feathers are the best stuffing feathers for anything, because as soon as you stuff them in they double, making it double-stuffed and double-fluffy!)

Finally, to create the snowflake pattern on its back, Santa wobbled to the window, opened it and scooped up a handful of real, un-meltable North Pole snow. North Pole snow is one of the most beautiful substances on the planet if you can stop it melting . . . and Santa can! He gently sprinkled the flakes over the back of the stuffed dinosaur and as they settled there the elves applauded in amazement.

The stuffed dinosaur was an almost perfect replica of the Christmasaurus. For some of the elves with poor eyesight, it looked as though there were two dinosaurs in the room!

For the Christmasaurus, this was the closest he'd ever come to looking at another dinosaur. For the first time in his life, he could imagine what it would be like if he weren't on his own. If he weren't so different.

He could imagine what it would be like to have a dinosaur friend.

Chapter Thirteen

THE NIGHT BEFORE THE NIGHT BEFORE CHRISTMAS

O n the night before the night before Christmas, it was A.S.H. (*all systems ho*) in the North Pole. The chocolates inside Advent calendars had almost disappeared, and all the elves were making final festive preparations. Everyone was incredibly excited about Christmas – everyone except for the Christmasaurus.

Not only was the Christmasaurus not excited about Christmas but he was actually wishing Christmas wouldn't come at all. He knew that on Christmas Eve Santa would be taking something very special away from him and giving it to some *spoilt little boy called William* (as the Christmasaurus thought of him).

Since the night he'd first laid eyes on Santa's wonderful stuffed dinosaur toy, the Christmasaurus had taken it with him wherever he went. He'd even given the cuddly dinosaur a name – Stuffy!

He'd taken Stuffy to the ice-skating rink and held its hand as they glided around on the ice together.

He'd spent hours and hours showing Stuffy his favourite Christmas movies in the North Pole cinema.

He'd taken Stuffy to meet the fairies and the snowmen.

He'd shown Stuffy how to roar under the Northern Lights.

And, best of all, they'd sat together watching the reindeer fly.

In the Christmasaurus's mind he had finally found a new dinosaur friend. For the first time, he wasn't the

only one! They were completely inseparable.

But that was about to change.

That night, the elves were manically wrapping presents, frantically loading them into sacks and panically piling them on to Santa's unbelievably enormous sleigh. The sound of frantic elf song echoed constantly around the North Pole as they continually sang the same song over and over and over again, which they did on this night every year. Santa had grown so sick of hearing it that he'd gone to the trouble of making himself some special earplugs that were

specifically designed to block out the sound of this particular elf song! Santa privately thought these were the best things he'd ever made, as they meant that he no longer had to listen to this:

It's the night before the night before Christmas,
The worst night of the year.
There's far too much to do
And it fills us up with fear.
It doesn't look like we'll make it
But we've brought this on ourselves,
So if Christmas doesn't come,
You can blame the North Pole elves.

It's the night before the night before Christmas
And we're busier than ever before.
There are toys up to our eyeballs
And our hands and feet are sore.
But you don't hear us complaining –
We sing our troubles away –
Whilst harnessing up the reindeer
To the still-not-ready sleigh!

It's the night before the night before Christmas,
No time for toilet breaks.
We've got microscopic fingers
So we might make some mistakes.
But as long as the job gets finished,
And Santa gets on his way,
We'll be happier than the kiddies
Getting toys on Christmas Day!

Those are just three of the thirty-eight verses of that song which the elves wailed out at the top of their voices. It was quite unpleasant enough to have to sit through the entire thing once, let alone repeatedly until the job was finished!

This year, the worst thing about the song was that it meant the time had finally come for the Christmasaurus to say goodbye to Stuffy. Sprout and Snozzletrump came to collect it, but couldn't seem to find Stuffy or the Christmasaurus anywhere. They searched high and low, low and high, until eventually they found the Christmasaurus hiding with Stuffy behind a stack of hay in the flying-reindeer stables.

The Christmasaurus let out a soft, sad roar and a large, dino-sized teardrop formed and froze on his scaly cheek as the elves slid his stuffed friend out from its hay hiding place.

Snozzletrump felt so sorry for the Christmasaurus. He could see just how much this toy meant to him. Even though the Christmasaurus had so many wonderful friends in the North Pole, none of them were dinosaurs, and Snozzletrump knew that was tough.

> 'I'm sorry, Christmasaurus,
> It's time to say goodbye.
> It's going somewhere special
> So there's no need for you to cry.
> It'll be loved and cherished
> Just the way it was by you
> But a little boy called William
> Needs a friend more than you do!'

whispered Snozzletrump as he patted and stroked the Christmasaurus.

The elves gave the Christmasaurus a hug and took

him back to his favourite spot by the fireside in Santa's dreaming den, where he curled up into a sad ball. They softly sang him a lullaby until he stopped crying and fell asleep, then they quietly took Stuffy away. It was swiftly wrapped in spotty paper with a red ribbon, and a tag was tied to it that said:

For William, From Santa

It was then put into a sack and heaved into the sleigh by four singing elves, along with thousands and thousands of other sacks.

As the night before the night before Christmas went on, the sleigh was piled with more and more sacks until they were stacked as high as a house, maybe even higher! If you saw it, you would say to yourself, '*That sleigh will never fly!*' However, the elves had a clever way of fixing that problem. Once the last sack had been heaved on to the sleigh, fifty fat farmer elves climbed up the mountain of toy sacks until they were on top of it, and started jumping up and down. It looked as though the elves were having some sort of silly sack-summit party high above the sleigh, but under their feet something magical was happening.

The sacks were squishing and shrinking down into the back of the sleigh. With each fat elf jump, the sacks squished more and more until, after an hour of jumping, the sleigh looked as if it only had one large bulging sack in the back, which fitted nice and neatly into the cargo area behind where Santa would soon sit.

The elves cheered and whooped and gave each other high-threes as all their preparations were finished. The night before the night before Christmas was nearly over, and all that was left to do now was get some rest. The elves blew out all the lanterns and candles so the Magnificently Magical Flying Reindeer could get some final shut-eye whilst they were harnessed to the sleigh. Everyone lay down on the floor all around the giant sleigh, and in no more than two seconds fell fast asleep.

CHAPTER FOURTEEN

A SECRET PASSENGER!

It was still the night before the night before Christmas, and all through the North Pole not a creature was stirring . . . except a dinosaur!

The Christmasaurus woke up suddenly next to the fire, which had now died down to its last glowing embers. Feeling cold and lonely, he looked around the room and could just make out the enormous belly of Santa as he lay asleep on his super-duper double-fatty kingsize bed.

Oh, how he wished that his stuffed dinosaur friend were still with him.

He knew that out there, somewhere, was someone who needed it more than he did, but that didn't make saying goodbye any easier.

Suddenly, an idea popped into the Christmasaurus's brain. It was a cheeky, naughty little idea, but once one of those ideas pops inside your head, it is almost impossible to pop it out again.

What if, he thought to himself, what if he were to just take one last peep at Stuffy, just to say one last little goodbye? He knew the toy was in the back of the sleigh somewhere. Surely it couldn't be that hard to find? And if he didn't do it *now* then he'd never get to see it again!

The Christmasaurus couldn't bear the thought of not having one last look. Quickly and quietly, he hopped up on to his feet and crept out of Santa's room. He didn't stop creeping until he was standing in the enormous barn they called the Sleigh Room at the foot of the enormous sleigh, surrounded by dozens of piles of exhausted sleeping elves (who were snoring in harmony).

Before he could think twice – he barely even thought

once! – he was climbing up the side of Santa's mighty sleigh. He'd never touched the sleigh before. It was so preciously shiny and special that to look at it was satisfying enough. But now he only had one thing on his mind – finding Stuffy!

He dived nose-first into the sea of sacks that filled the back of the sleigh. He swam deeper into the prickly fabric. He sniffed around through sacks of soldiers, cars and trucks, dollies and ponies . . . but that stuffed dinosaur was packed deep! So, deeper the Christmasaurus went, until suddenly his little dinosaur claws felt something.

Yes, that was it! He recognized the cuddly squish of his stuffed friend.

The Christmasaurus clawed his way inside the sack and poked his nose through a tiny gap in the wrapping paper, until his wonderful icy eyes were staring into the golden buttons of Stuffy.

The Christmasaurus gave Stuffy one last hug goodbye.

It was a long hug.

A very long hug.

So long, in fact, that before the Christmasaurus knew what was happening, he was drifting happily back off to sleep . . .

A Secret Passenger!

CLANG!

The Christmasaurus woke with a start. The room outside the sleigh no longer sounded snoozy and quiet. It was now full of the busy sounds of elf feet scurrying in every direction, polishing the brass skis on the sleigh, jangling every sleigh bell on the reindeers' reins and replacing any that had lost their jingle.

The Christmasaurus had slept in the back of the sleigh all night . . . It was now Christmas Eve!

'Good morning, my teensy, busy little elves!' boomed Santa's voice. By the sound of his heavy bootsteps, the Christmasaurus knew Santa was already dressed in his Christmas Eve suit, a gloriously long, quilted red flying jacket with extra pockets for cookies and fudge brownies, his black fireproof boots and a red hat with a fluffy white bobble. The Christmasaurus peered through a gap in the sacks of presents. Santa looked outstandingly large and jolly.

'Good morning, Santa, the sleigh is set!
You're ready to fly but don't forget
That under your seat is a spare red hat
And if you feel tired then take a nap!'

the elves sang in unison as Santa climbed up into the front of the sleigh.

The Christmasaurus was trapped!

If he climbed out now, then he would surely be seen, and Santa would know that he'd snuck a sneaky peek in the sleigh and crumpled a perfectly elf-wrapped present! That was extremely naughty indeed!

But if he stayed where he was, then he'd be stuck flying around the world with the reindeer in Santa's sleigh.

Flying around the world with the reindeer in Santa's sleigh?

Flying . . .

Reindeer . . .

Sleigh . . .

That had been the Christmasaurus's dream since the day he'd laid eyes upon those flying deer! Was this his chance to experience what flying like a reindeer was *really* like? Or should he climb out of the sleigh and come clean?

Before he could decide what to do, there was a sudden jolt that rattled the sleigh. The great barn doors had just been opened and the Magnificently Magical Flying Reindeer were tugging at the reins, ready to rocket into the sky.

'My elves!' Santa called from the front seat of his sleigh.

> 'My tiny elves, my little friends,
> Your work is almost done.
> Now I must do my duty
> To deliver every one
> Of all these gifts and goodies
> To every girl and boy,
> Fill each and every stocking
> With each and every toy.
> So I'll fly into the sky
> Behind this herd of magic deer
> To house and home and rooftop
> Just as I do each year

'And when all the sacks are empty,
Not one left to deliver,
We'll head back through the sky
For we'll have no more need to shiver.
We'll celebrate tomorrow
With mince pies and candy canes
And start dreaming about next year
When it's Christmastime again!'

Santa lifted his arms in the air and there was a sudden hush. An intensely magical silence flooded the great barn. The cold, crisp air that was blowing through the open barn doors suddenly stopped too, and the snowflakes that had found their way inside hung suspended in the air as if time itself had slowed down.

Santa was smiling to himself, and somewhere in the pile of toys behind him the Christmasaurus was secretly wagging his tail. Was he actually about to experience flying?

Each of the reindeer that was strapped up to the sleigh now had its eyes fixed on Santa, waiting for him to give the sign. Then, just before time seemed to stop completely, Santa reached inside his enormous coat and pulled something quite bizarre out of the inside pocket. It was a full-sized, old-fashioned gramophone – a record player with an enormously curly brass horn. Quite how it fitted inside his coat pocket I'll never know! Santa placed it softly on the seat next to him in the sleigh. Then he took off his red hat, reached inside it and pulled out a vinyl record! He carefully placed it on to the turntable, lowered the needle into the first, fine groove and flicked a little brass switch on the side. Music exploded out of the enormous brassy horn and filled the room with song.

Music is a magic like no other, which can do incredible, unexplainable things. Suddenly, the heavy skis of Santa's sleigh lifted up a centimetre or two off the barn floor, as though they were floating on the music itself.

Then Santa gave the sign, and he started singing!

'I heard a noise on the rooftop!
It made my heart go jump!
The stomp of boots and the clop of hooves
Went clippedy, clippedy, clump!
Oh, I heard a noise on the rooftop!
I wonder what it was . . .
I really ho, ho, hope it's Santa Claus!'

The reindeer launched into a gallop and whooshed through the giant barn doors!

'I heard a noise on the rooftop!
It sounded like a sleigh . . .'

Santa continued, singing his favourite Christmas song, accompanied by the magic orchestra blasting from the gramophone:

'I went to bed on Christmas Eve,
and soon it's Christmas Day . . .'

A Secret Passenger!

The Christmasaurus rattled and bounced and rolled around in the back of the sleigh with the biggest grin on his scaly face, still clinging on to the arms of William's stuffed dinosaur.

'Oh, I heard a noise on the rooftop!
Now I can't sleep because . . .'

Then the thud of glowing golden galloping deer hooves on the snow stopped . . . They weren't thudding on snow any more. They were galloping on the air itself.

They were flying.

The sleigh was flying.

Santa was flying.

The Christmasaurus was flying!

'I really ho, ho, hope it's Santa Claus!' warbled Santa with a jolly smile as the sleigh and its secret passenger disappeared into the Northern Lights towards the waiting world.

Chapter Fifteen
THE HUNTER

It was Christmas Eve and William was getting ready for bed unusually early (as all children should on Christmas Eve!), but not before placing a mince pie for the reindeer and a carrot for Santa on the wonky little wooden table by the chimney. I bet you thought Santa eats the mince pies and the reindeer eat the carrots, but that's 'The most common Christmas Eve mistake!' as Mr Trundle would knowingly say each year.

Mr Trundle tucked William into bed and, although he desperately wanted to stay awake for as long as possible, he was so worn out with Christmas excitement he fell fast asleep within 0.8 seconds of his head touching his pillow. William managed to stay awake a little longer, but eventually they were both fast asleep.

As William lay snoozing, dreaming Christmassy dreams in his head, he was completely unaware that those tiny little hairs on his arms and his neck were all standing on end again.

They were standing on end again because William was still being watched.

Outside, it had been snowing heavily all day. All the rooftops in William's street were thickly coated in white freezing fluff that was as smooth as the icing on a Christmas cake – all except one rooftop, whose perfectly fallen snow had been disturbed by something. Two sets of footprints were scattered around the roof, drawing large circles in the snow. *Someone* was there and, judging by the hundreds of steps, they must have been pacing back and forth for quite some time.

The owners of these footprints were a man and his dog, but they weren't pacing any more. They were as still as statues, hiding behind the chimney!

But what were a man and a dog doing on the rooftop

opposite William's house on Christmas Eve? Why had they been spying on William for the past few weeks? And why were they now sitting out of sight in the freezing snow? Who were they?

Well, I will tell you.

This man was **evil**.

This man was *the Hunter*.

THE HUNTER

The Hunter was an old man with creased, leathery skin on his face and a large, lumpy, white scar that ran from his eye down to his chin. He wore a very odd-looking hunting hat with a long peacock feather sticking proudly out of it (the poor peacock's head was now the handle of an umbrella!) and he was always smoking a crooked pipe made of ivory, even in his sleep. Its sickly, bitter smoke hung in the air for hours, and if you were standing next to him the smoke would sting your nostrils most unpleasantly.

The most obvious thing about him, though, was just how incredibly posh he was. He looked posh. Smelt posh. Walked and talked posh. Even the way he was crouched behind the chimney was posh! In fact, he was so posh that his socks were made of pure gold thread, and he only blew his nose on real ten pound notes!

The Hunter was the eldest son of a very wealthy man, and when his father died, the Hunter inherited piles and piles of family gold. He kept it all to himself in a huge vault inside the family mansion and refused

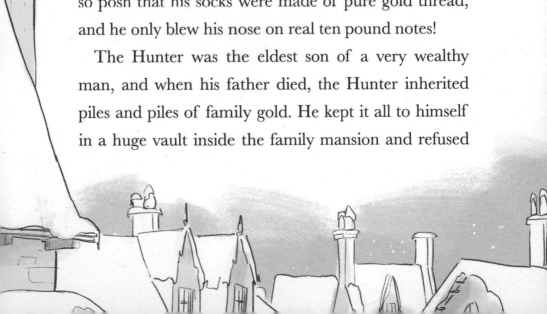

to let anyone else inside. He shut himself away from his family. From the world. Even the annual Christmas cards from distant relatives couldn't drag him away from counting his wealth.

He loved money.

He loved gold.

But most of all he loved *hunting*.

He started hunting poor, innocent animals when he was a little boy. Whilst his filthy-rich parents were away on long exotic holidays, he would be left at home with his nanny who was too busy looking after his *perfect* baby brother to pay him any attention.

First, he hunted the neighbours' cat with a trap made of leftover chopsticks (the ones that no one ever uses) from Chinese takeaways.

He enjoyed it so much that the next day he set his pet hamster free in the garden-hedge maze, then hunted it down with a slingshot made from the neighbours' cat's bones.

Then he released his goldfish into the moat and hunted it using a snooker cue from the billiard room as a spear.

THE HUNTER

Back then, when he was little, the Hunter was known as Huxley. But one long winter holiday at home from boarding school he managed to track and hunt every single animal in a twelve-mile radius of the family mansion. From then on he became known only as *the Hunter.*

Huxley was no more.

Over the years, the animals he liked to hunt had become more and more exotic, and the more rare the animal the more he wanted to kill it!

He'd hunted lions and tigers. Bears and monkeys. Zebras and giraffes. But they weren't anywhere near rare enough for the Hunter any more. He liked to hunt the *really* ridiculously rare animals, creatures so rare that most people have never heard of them (but they're all very real).

He had the horn of a unicorn, which he'd hunted in the glaciers of Greenland.

He had the paw of a pink polar bear he'd shot with a crossbow at the foot of a rainbow.

He had the ears of a pandaroo, the gills of a horseshark, the tail of a snailwhale, the tongue of a fanglebeast, the snout of a pigfish and the wings of twenty thousand flying ants he'd swatted in Sweden on Flying Ant Day.

He hunted creatures of all sorts and once he'd shot them he had their heads mounted on the walls of his great mansion.

Wherever the Hunter went, his loyal dog, Growler, followed. Growler had been the Hunter's trusty companion for many, many years. He did anything the Hunter told him to – because if he didn't he knew he would end up as a head on the mansion wall!

But why were the Hunter and Growler hiding on a rooftop in the snow on Christmas Eve, and why had they been secretly spying on William for the past few weeks?

Well, I was just about to tell you before you interrupted me!

You see, one Christmas Eve a very long time ago,

when the Hunter was still called Huxley, he had seen the most fantastic sight any boy could ever see. He had seen a flying reindeer.

His younger brother had heard something in the sky over the mansion: someone was *singing*. Then all of a sudden a gigantic sleigh had burst through a break in the snow clouds. The little boy had called for his brother, and that's when Huxley had seen them . . . nine Magnificently Magical Flying Reindeer.

Flying reindeer!

FLYING reindeer!!!

'By golly gosh!' Huxley had said. 'Flying reindeer? I don't believe my eyes!'

'They have to be the rarest creatures in the world!' exclaimed Huxley's little brother.

And they were.

'I *must* have one!' Huxley had cried.

From that night on, the Hunter's life had changed. All he thought about, all he wanted, was the head of a Magnificently Magical Flying Reindeer hanging on his wall above his fireplace. It was all he dreamt about.

Ever since that night, he had focused all his hunting efforts on tracking Santa down to get a clear shot at one of those rare creatures. And a few weeks ago, he had seen something that gave him a wickedly evil idea. A young, sad boy, sitting in a wheelchair, with his ridiculously festively dressed father.

It was William!

'Look at this boy here, Growler, that useless lump of sadness in that wheelchair,' the Hunter said to his dog. 'Hmmmm . . . a young, sad boy in a wheelchair. Tut, tut, how very pathetic . . .' he continued with a cunning smile growing on his face.

The Hunter had had an idea.

'By golly gosh, Growler, I do believe I know how to find those flying reindeer!' he cried with an evil twinkle in his posh black eyes. 'We've been trying to find them for all these years, but we've been doing it all wrong, my furry fiend!' He thumped his dog on the back with horrid excitement. 'We need to let Santa bring those fantastic flying beasties to *us*! Don't you see, you stupid mutt? How could Santa possibly NOT pay this poor, pathetic boy a visit this Christmas? Of course he will! You idiotic little fleabag, don't you understand? We'll follow this boy, set up camp on the roof and wait until Christmas Eve. Santa will swoop down from the sky on that garish sleigh of his, and when he slides down this boy's chimney, those magical deer of his will be left all alone, in plain sight! *That's* when I'll do it. I'll shoot them, Growler. I'll shoot them all!' The Hunter let out a cackle as he rubbed his greedy hands together with delight at the thought of shooting Santa's flying reindeer. 'We'll finally have them, the heads of the rarest creatures on the planet, hanging on our glorious wall above the fireplace!'

He let out an almighty maniacal laugh. Growler just huffed out a sigh of relief, thankful that he was a dog and not a flying reindeer!

So, the Hunter and his dog followed William to his home, staying hidden in the shadows. They watched his every movement. They saw him get creamed at the supermarket. They were waiting inside the postbox. And now they were sitting on the rooftop opposite

William's wonky little house, waiting for Santa's sleigh to appear, for tonight was Christmas Eve. Tonight the Hunter would shoot the Magnificently Magical Flying Reindeer!

CHAPTER SIXTEEN

THE RAREST CREATURE ON THE PLANET

Everything was still. The Hunter and his dog Growler stared out across a snowy, white desert of empty rooftops, keeping their sights firmly set on one in particular: William Trundle's.

At midnight, a chime from the town clock tower echoed through the streets, filling the air with a loud **CLONG** ... *then another ... and another ...* It was almost time. The Hunter could feel it in his evil bones. Growler sensed it too as he shuffled nervously in their snowy hideout.

Suddenly everything seemed to stop.

The snow stopped falling. It just hung in the air as if someone had pressed pause.

The chimes of the clock tower had stopped early too.

Time seemed to be standing still.

Santa had arrived.

The enormous sleigh burst out of the clouds with such a clatter it's surprising the entire town didn't wake up at the jingle of sleigh bells and the Christmas carols blasting out of the swirly brass horn of Santa's gramophone.

The Hunter's beady, greedy eyes lit up as the rarest creatures on the planet swooped directly over his head. He could have reached up and touched them if he'd dared, but that would have given the game away, and if he wanted their heads to hang on his wall then he needed to stay hidden.

THE RAREST CREATURE ON THE PLANET

The Hunter cracked his gnarly knuckles and tightened his grip round his most prized possession: a fully shot-o-matic, high precision, bangerific, lethal sniper rifle. It was an awful machine for an awful man and he never left home without it, even if he was just popping out to buy milk! It had a long barrel that was so straight you could use it as a ruler, and on top was a telescopic sight so powerful that if you looked down it on a clear day you could see all the way round the world until you saw the back of your own head.

Santa circled the sleigh above the town a few times, making sure he'd found exactly the right house. (He's been known to make some mistakes in the past!)

Finally, he landed the sleigh on William's rooftop. It was a smooth landing, although the roof was a tight squeeze for such a large sleigh and a herd of galloping reindeer.

The Hunter couldn't take his eyes off them. There they were, the creatures he'd been dreaming about for what felt like his whole life.

'Oh my . . .' he whispered to Growler. 'They're even more magnificent than I remember!' And they really were. 'Now get out of your sleigh, fatty, and disappear down that chimney!' the Hunter muttered under his breath as he watched Santa climb down from the sleigh.

'Oh, what a wonderful night!' cried Santa to his deer. 'Lovely soft landing, that was, my dear deers. Well done! Jolly smooth indeed. I can tell you've been practising hard. Pays off when you get a wonky little roof like this. Doesn't leave much room for error.'

But the deer weren't paying attention to Santa. They were sniffing the air. Something smelt funny. Something was stinging their nostrils. It was smoke.

Pipe smoke!

The deer grunted and shuffled nervously, but Santa paid no notice to them.

'Oh, hush down, my dearies. I won't be a minute, and then we'll be back up in the clouds!' Santa said as he shuffled round to the back of the sleigh and reached in with one arm to retrieve William's gift. 'Where . . . is . . . it?' he said as he fumbled around. 'Aha! Here it is!'

He gave it a tug, but it didn't want to budge. He tugged it again, but it stayed put, almost as if something were pulling at it from the other end. 'Hmmm, that's very odd!' he said as he tried one last time. He put his big, black, shiny boot on the lip of the sleigh and pulled with all his might. *Pop!* It came free and the dinosaur-shaped package flew out of the sleigh and into Santa's arms.

Santa gave a little chuckle and plodded over to the chimney. Then something very strange happened. It was almost as if the entire world grew very large all of a sudden whilst Santa remained the same size! Faster than you can say jingle bells, everything grew: the rooftop, the sleigh, the sky, the reindeer, the house and especially the chimney. They all blew up like massive, magical balloons, but Santa stayed exactly as he was before.

Now that everything was extra-large, Santa was just the right size to plop his fat belly into the mammoth hole in the top of the chimney and slide down it with ease.

The Hunter was dumbfounded. He'd never seen such magic before. It gave him the spooks! He quickly forgot about that, though, for he suddenly realized that the time had come. The moment he'd been waiting for. His horrid plan was working perfectly!

He raised his heavy, deadly, sniper rifle until

the super-zoom scope was pressed firmly against his bloodshot eyeball. Down the telescopic sight he could see, sitting perfectly still, eight Magnificently Magical Flying Reindeer. They were in plain sight, clear as day – sitting ducks! He put his long, posh finger round the cold metallic trigger and lined up the crosshair in his sight.

'It's almost too easy!' the Hunter whispered to Growler. 'Even *you* could take this shot!'

He took a deep puff of the pipe that hung from his chapped lips and held his breath for a moment to steady his aim. He squinted down the sight and a tear of evil excitement plopped over his bottom eyelid and ran down his scarred cheek.

'I finally have you . . .'

But as his finger tightened on the trigger, just before he took the shot, the Hunter saw *something*. Something was moving in the back of the sleigh!

'What the devil?' he said as he realigned his scope to get a better look at what was causing the commotion. Toy sacks were bumping around, bobbing up and down as if something were underneath them!

And that's when he saw it. A shiny, blue, scaly head popped up from the sacks.

'I d-d-d-don't believe my eyes . . .' the Hunter stuttered as his pipe dropped from his open, gobsmacked mouth. He was staring at a real, living –

'D-D-D-DINOSAUR?'

The Hunter's life had once again changed for ever. Everything he'd thought he wanted he suddenly didn't want any more.

'A real, living dinosaur! Growler, do you know what this *means*?' the Hunter said frantically as he wiped the lenses on his sniper-rifle scope and had a second, third and fourth look, just to check that what he was seeing was real. 'Take a look, you stupid hound!' he said, shoving the scope into Growler's eye.

'Those reindeer mean nothing to me now . . . Look, there's a rooftop full of them! Hardly what you would call *rare*!' he said as he yanked back the rifle to get another look for himself. 'But there's only ONE dinosaur! That scaly, blue oversized animal over there is without doubt *the rarest creature on the planet*! The only one in the world, and I *must* have his head on my wall! *Why*, if I had the head of that dinosaur on my wall, I would be famous! I'd go down in hunting history. I'd be . . . *The Greatest Hunter of All Time*!'

At that moment, he tightened his grip on his rifle and took aim at the dinosaur.

But the dinosaur was moving around fast. The Hunter realized that he was sniffing the snow, searching for something. He jumped from one side of the sleigh to the other, sniffing the footprints, ducking in and out of the reindeer's legs. He was a tricky, moving target for the Hunter, who had no experience of shooting dinosaurs.

'Keep still, you little . . .' the Hunter mumbled as he climbed out of his hiding place on the rooftop and moved to get a better shot. He walked round the chimney, trying to keep the dinosaur in his sight.

The Hunter took one step and the dinosaur skipped behind the sleigh.

The Hunter took another step and the dinosaur hopped up on to the ledge of the chimney.

The Hunter took one more step and . . .

SWOOOOOSH!

BANG!

The Hunter stepped right off the edge of the rooftop and fell ten metres into the bushes below with a thud, sending a gunshot ringing up into the sky. He'd been so transfixed by the dinosaur that he'd failed to realize he had been walking towards the edge of the roof.

The sound of the Hunter's sky-bound gunshot made the Christmasaurus jump so hard that he lost his footing on the edge of the chimney and slipped right into the magically inflated hole. He fell down the chimney flue, into the sooty darkness of the fireplace.

The Christmasaurus was in William's home!

Chapter Seventeen

A Dinosaur in the House

The Christmasaurus landed with a crash in the fireplace. Luckily, the fire hadn't been lit, because Mr Trundle knew that you should *never* light your fire on Christmas Eve. The dinosaur got to his feet and stepped out into William's empty living room.

The Christmasaurus had never been in a room like this before. He'd only ever known the large, oversized, magical rooms of the North Pole ranch, and they were far grander than this wonky little room. But there was something he instantly liked about it. Something felt cosy. Warm. Happy. He could sense that the people who lived here were full of love.

But there wasn't time to look around. He was desperate to see Stuffy one last time. He had to find his toy, say goodbye and get back up to the sleigh before Santa caught him. He was being *very* naughty! His dinosaur eyes scanned the room, searching for any sign of the spotty wrapping paper or shiny red ribbon. But there was nothing. There was a small Christmas tree, about the size of an elf (he'd never seen one so tiny before), which had a scattering of small presents underneath it, but none of them were Stuffy.

Santa must have put it in William's room! The Christmasaurus knew that Santa did that sometimes. So he tiptoed out of the living room, sniffing the beige patterned carpet, following the scent of Santa (who smelt like fresh mint chocolate and tangerines). The door to the next room was slightly ajar, and through the crack the Christmasaurus could just make out the shape of a small bed. Sitting in a sliver of a moonbeam on the bedroom floor was the beautifully wrapped dinosaur-shaped present for which he was searching.

He slipped inside William's bedroom, but paused for a moment to take in all the wonderful dinosaur pictures and toys and books and posters and wallpaper . . . He'd never seen so much dinosaur stuff before.

It was **dinosawesome!**

A Dinosaur in the House

As his eyes circled the room, they came back to Stuffy, perfectly wrapped on the bedroom floor. He crept across the room as carefully as he could until he was face to face with where the stuffed dinosaur's nose would be. Through a small slit in the wrapping paper he could just make out the soft glow of the toy's golden button eyes, staring out.

The Christmasaurus took a deep breath. This was it. This was goodbye. Goodbye to the first and only dinosaur friend he'd ever had. He gave it a crumpled hug through the wrapping paper, and over its cuddly shoulder he saw William lying snugly asleep in his bed.

It was at that moment that the Christmasaurus suddenly felt a funny feeling in his tummy, like the sinking sort of feeling you get when you drive over a bridge really fast. He glanced around the room at the photos of William and Mr Trundle, then at the empty wheelchair next to the bed. He huffed a deep sigh through his nostrils and then straightened up the present so it looked as close to elf-perfect as possible. It was time to let Stuffy go.

That's when he heard it.

FLUSH!
STOMP!
STOMP!

It was the unmistakable sound of the toilet flushing,

followed by Santa's boots, stomping speedily down the hallway.

STOMP!

STOMP!

STOMP!

He was marching faster and the Christmasaurus saw his jolly round shadow pass William's bedroom door.

Santa was already in the living room!

'Ooh, a carrot! My favourite!' he heard Santa whisper before crunching into his treat.

The Christmasaurus panicked. If he didn't make it back up on to the roof before Santa, then he would be . . . *left behind*!

He turned clumsily on the spot, and with a thud his long tail swung round behind him, knocking off every book on William's bookshelf (all books about dinosaurs, of course!). Then he took a great leap towards the door, but his clunky dinosaur claws got caught in Stuffy's wrapping ribbon, and the Christmasaurus went tumble-bumbling across to the other side of the bedroom, smash-whacking into the wardrobe.

A Dinosaur in the House

As you can imagine, this made such a clatter that William woke up in an instant.

'W . . . wh . . . what's going . . . on?' he said through a yawn, rubbing his sleepy eyes open.

As the room came into focus, William saw a large, spotty present sitting beyond the foot of his bed, hand-tied with a red ribbon. But the ribbon had come undone. His eyes followed the loose red ribbon along the floor until it reached a large, scaly, foot. The ribbon was caught round the Christmasaurus's claw, all tangled in knots! Before William could blink, before he could scream, before he could think, before he could even do anything whatsoever, the Christmasaurus bolted out of the room at a hundred miles an hour, dragging the present behind him. William scrambled out of bed into his waiting wheelchair and chased after them!

The Christmasaurus burst into the small, cosy living room just in time to see Santa's big black boots disappear magically up the chimney. He roared a panicked roar and dived towards the fireplace, trampling over presents and tripping over the miniature Christmas tree in the process, sending decorations flying through the air and scattering over the floor! But that didn't stop the Christmasaurus. He crawled into the fireplace and looked up the chimney, which now seemed far too small for even an elf to get through! He tried desperately to jump, climb and claw his way up it, but it was no use. Santa's magic had worn off, and the chimney flue had deflated back to its normal size.

Then came the worst noise of all. The clopping of hooves accompanied by soft Christmas music echoed down the chimney, then all of a sudden seemed to disappear completely. The Christmasaurus let out a howl-like roar up the chimney into the sky above – but it was too late.

They had gone.

The Christmasaurus had been left behind.

It was at that moment that a bright, round light switched on like a spotlight. It was a shaky, wobbly light. It was coming from a torch in William's nervous hands as he sat in his wheelchair at the doorway, looking at a dinosaur in his home.

CHAPTER EIGHTEEN
A BOY AND A DINOSAUR

They stayed perfectly still. Staring at each other. William and the Christmasaurus. A boy and a dinosaur, face to face for the first time in history. Neither of them knew what to do or say.

Then suddenly William let out a frightened

'AaaaaAAARGH!'

And the Christmasaurus released a scared

'RooooAAARGH!'

They both sat roaring and screaming at each other for what felt like the longest time, until eventually they both ran out of breath and stopped. They searched each other's faces and, although neither of them knew what they were searching for, they found that they were both just as frightened as each other, which suddenly made them not scared of each other at all. It's funny how things work like that.

'William? What's all that noise?' croaked a sleepy Mr Trundle from upstairs.

William looked into the dinosaur's big, frightened blue eyes.

'Nothing, Dad, just had a bad dream,' William replied in his best attempt at sounding casual.

There was a pause that seemed to last for ever.

'Oh . . . OK.' Mr Trundle yawned. 'Well, get some sleep or Santa won't come!' And with that William heard his dad's bedroom door close.

'H . . . hello?' William said quietly, as he wheeled himself slowly into the living room over the piles of festive debris that now decorated the floor. He rolled closer to the fireplace and he couldn't believe his eyes.

A Boy and a Dinosaur

There, right in front of him, was an actual, living, breathing, *dinosaur*! How was that possible? Not only that – he was the most awesome-looking dinosaur William had ever seen! He had smooth, icy scales and big blue eyes, like a wintery lion. But he was currently tangled from head to tail in ribbon and wrapping paper, tinsel and fairy lights. The dinosaur was decorated like a Christmas tree. As William got closer, he saw that there was a tag, very loosely stuck to the dinosaur's back. It said:

For William,
from Santa

'No way!' William whispered. 'I never in my wildest dreams thought Santa would bring me a *real* dinosaur!'

Suddenly he found the courage to reach out his hand to stroke the dinosaur. But just as his hand got to a millimetre away from the dinosaur's long, smooth nose, the creature turned to look at something through the window. William followed his gaze. Something small and red was zooming across the sky!

The Christmasaurus burst into a run once again, this time heading out of the living room towards the front door. He scrambled and skidded on all the decorations and bits of plastic Christmas tree, becoming more tangled as he went. Suddenly William felt a sharp *yank* and his wheelchair spun round on the spot.

'*Oh no . . . wait!*' he screamed.

He looked down and saw that the other end of the fairy lights and tinsel that were wrapped around the dinosaur had become tangled around his wheelchair.

He was *attached* to the dinosaur!

His wheelchair lurched forward as he was suddenly dragged across the living room and into the hallway. All William could do was hold on for dear life as the panicked and determined dinosaur launched full speed ahead, towards the front door.

'Stop! Wait!' cried William. 'The front door is locked!'

But that didn't matter. The Christmasaurus bowed his hard, scaly head and in one massive

BAM!

he burst through the door, pulling William and his wheelchair through the dinosaur-shaped hole and into the snowy street!

The Christmasaurus searched the sky for Santa's sleigh as he ran. It was cloudy now and difficult to see anything, but *there* it was! Just for a split second it poked through a break in the clouds, shiny and red, zooming through the sky. It must have been moonlight reflecting on the red paint of the sleigh! He gave chase, sprinting as fast as his dinosaur legs would carry him, littering the streets with broken baubles that were flying off from the strings tangled around his body.

He skidded round the icy corners with William whizzing along behind him. William used the brakes on his wheelchair to avoid lampposts, parked cars, postboxes and the occasional cat as they accelerated through the town.

The Christmasaurus couldn't see the sleigh any more – it was above the snow clouds and getting away. There was only one thing for it, thought the Christmasaurus, he was going to have to . . . fly!

He'd seen the reindeer do it a million times. He'd spent his whole life dreaming of flying and tonight was *his* night . . . He could feel it! He put his head down low and started a strange, reindeer-like gallop.

'What . . . are . . . you . . . doing?' cried William as he got a faceful of snow, kicked up by the crazed dinosaur. He brushed the snow from his eyes just in time to see the Christmasaurus take a deep breath, his strides getting longer and higher, higher and longer!

Then, at the side of the road, the Christmasaurus spotted some sort of ramp that was being used for roadworks – it was a perfect takeoff ramp!

The Christmasaurus headed straight for the ramp and galloped up it as fast as he could, his eyes set on his target: the sky!

William couldn't believe what he was seeing.

This dinosaur is bonkers!

He doesn't have wings.

He isn't a reindeer.

He can't fly! William thought to himself as he held on tight to the armrests of his wheelchair, too scared to let go to buckle his seatbelt.

As the dinosaur reached the end of the ramp he took an almighty leap into the air, pulling William in his wheelchair off the ground . . .

SMAAAA AASH!

They came crashing down in a pile of rubble, sending a mixture of dust and Christmas sparkles into the air. William only just managed to keep his chair from tipping over!

A Boy and a Dinosaur

They didn't fly. Just as William had thought.

As the glittery dust settled, the clouds parted for a moment, just long enough for them to see the red flashing lights of an aeroplane fly overhead. It wasn't the sleigh after all. The Christmasaurus let out a sad, lost roar and William put his arm out and gave him a comforting stroke. It was the first time he'd ever touched a dinosaur.

His skin was bumpy but smooth at the same time. Warm but also cool. Magical!

'Were you trying to fly?' William asked.

The Christmasaurus nodded, ashamed that he'd failed.

'Oh . . . I'm really sorry, but I don't believe dinosaurs like *you* can fly!' William said.

The Christmasaurus looked sad. Something about William's words seemed to hurt. William saw that he was upset and instinctively put his arms round the dinosaur's strong, solid neck and gave him a hug.

'It's OK. I know how you feel,' whispered William, and he gently stroked the dinosaur's head.

That was the moment that William and the Christmasaurus became friends.

But the boy and the dinosaur had something else in common: they'd both just heard a noise. Someone else was in the street with them!

CHAPTER NINETEEN

BUMPING INTO BRENDA

They both froze and fell dead silent. Who else could possibly be out in the street in the middle of the night on Christmas Eve? A **sniffle-sniffle** sort of sound broke through the cold quiet air. They heard it again and both knew that there was *definitely* someone else nearby!

'Who . . . who's there?' called William nervously, hoping that no one would reply. The Christmasaurus backed up like a scared puppy until he was almost sitting on William's lap! Then they heard it again: **sniffle-sniffle!**

Someone was crying!

'Hello? Are you OK?' William said kindly in the direction of the sniffly sobs. They seemed to be coming from behind a small bush in the garden of the house in front of which they were standing.

'D . . . d . . . don't . . . come . . . any closer! Or . . . I'll smash your face in!' snapped a snotty, stuffy voice from behind the leaves.

William recognized her voice at once. It was the last person he'd ever want to bump into . . . Brenda Payne!

'Quick, get out of sight!' William whispered to the Christmasaurus. He didn't want Brenda getting a glimpse of his new dinosaur – he had to stay a secret!

But this wasn't the Brenda that William was used to. He'd never, ever, EV-ER seen Brenda Payne cry before. He didn't know Brenda had any feelings other than anger, hate and horribleness . . . This was something he *had* to see with his own eyes!

'Are you crying?' William asked as he wheeled himself across the snowy pavement towards Brenda's front gate.

'What are you doing? Go away! I'm . . . sniff . . . completely . . . sniffle . . . fine!' snapped Brenda.

198

BUMPING INTO BRENDA

'OK!' William shrugged, but just as he was about to wheel himself away something stopped him. His wheelchair wouldn't budge. He tried to leave again, but he was stuck! Then he realized that he was still attached to the dinosaur by the strings of fairy lights and baubles and tinsel. His eyes followed them to where the dinosaur was standing and he saw a kind, caring sort of expression on the wonderfully scaly face.

The dinosaur couldn't speak, of course – at least, not like you and me – but he had feelings just the same, and sometimes feelings are loud enough to be understood better than any words. As William looked into the dinosaur's icy blue eyes, it was as though he could hear his thoughts as clearly as if he were speaking perfect English (with a slight North Pole accent, obviously).

The Christmasaurus huffed with his nose, criss-crossed his eyes and nodded his head in Brenda's direction, and William instantly knew what the dinosaur was saying:

GIRL. NEEDS. FRIEND.

William sighed. He hated to admit it, but the Christmasaurus was right. Every bone in his body wanted to get as far away from Brenda as possible but no one, not even Brenda *Snotty-Pants* Payne, deserved to be crying alone in their front garden on Christmas Eve.

'You stay!' William mouthed to the Christmasaurus, who immediately parked his bottom on the snowy street by Brenda's gate like an obedient dog, looking very happy with himself at managing to convince William to help the girl.

William unlooped the string of fairy lights from his chair, pushed open Brenda's gate and wheeled himself into her front garden. It was something he never thought he'd do! As he wheeled towards the sound of her sobs and sniffles, he glanced at her house. He'd seen her house many times before, but he usually whizzed by so fast, hoping she wouldn't see him, that he'd never paid much attention to it. Now, for the first time, he noticed that it stood out like a sore thumb amongst the other houses. Whichever way William looked down the street, every house was covered with some sort of Christmas decoration. Some had flashy, dancing lights, others just a simple wreath. William's, of course, had just about every Christmas decoration his dad could afford covering every inch of their wonky little house.

But Brenda's was completely bare. Dark. Cold. Utterly un-Christmassy.

Through the window William could see no sign of a Christmas tree, no Christmas cards at the fireplace, no wreath on the door and, most of all, no presents!

'Go ahead, laugh. I know you want to,' sobbed Brenda.

'I don't want to laugh at all,' said William truthfully. For William, seeing a house looking so *normal* at this time of year was a little creepy! 'Why don't you have any Christmas decorations?' he asked.

'If I tell you, you'll hate me,' said Brenda.

'I already hate you,' said William, 'so you might as well tell me!'

Brenda looked up at William and the corner of her mouth twitched into a tiny smile. William smiled back and they both let out a little laugh.

That was weird.

'Don't you *like* Christmas?' asked William.

'Of course I do! It's *her* . . .' Brenda said as she pointed at the figure of a woman pacing around inside the house.

William recognized her at once. It was the scroogy lady he and his dad had passed on their way to the postbox a few weeks ago. She was the most serious-looking woman William had ever seen, and had skin as pale as the moon. As William watched her, he noticed that she was ripping up pieces of paper.

'That's my mum,' said Brenda.

William gasped. Brenda's mum couldn't be any more the opposite of William's dad. She was dressed in old pyjamas, and her expression was more like she was heading to a funeral rather than Christmas Eve! Even though she seemed seriously serious, William could see instantly where Brenda got her annoyingly perfect prettiness from. Her mother was very beautiful – or at least she would have been if she didn't look so awfully sad. When William looked closer, he noticed that it wasn't paper she was ripping to shreds. They were Christmas cards!

'Why is she ripping up Christmas cards?' William asked.

'She . . . she . . .' Brenda struggled to get the words out. 'She hates Christmas!' And as she said it she scrunched up a perfectly round snowball in her hand and launched it at the front of her house.

'But why?' William asked. 'How can anyone hate Christmas? Does your dad hate it too?'

Brenda paused with her trembling hand full of a half-made snowball.

'What is it?' asked William, sensing that she was keeping something secret. He glanced quickly at the dinosaur peeping over the wall, who was staring encouragingly back at William.

William watched Brenda take a deep breath. Whatever she was about to say was obviously very difficult.

'I don't have a dad,' said Brenda. Just like that.

'Oh,' replied William.

'Well, I do have a dad, but I just don't see him any more,' Brenda explained. 'My mum and dad got divorced a year ago . . . one year ago *exactly*, on Christmas Eve.'

William looked up at the cold, dark, undecorated

house and began to understand.

'My mum used to love Christmas, but this year she says it just reminds her too much of Dad, so . . .' Brenda gulped hard and finished rolling the snowball. 'So this year she cancelled Christmas.'

As those awful words left her lips, a single teardrop formed in her eye and fell into the snowball she was holding. She quickly threw it at the wall and made another one.

William sat thinking about everything he'd just heard. For the first time ever, he actually felt sorry for Brenda Payne. Was this why she was the way she was? William imagined what he would be like if he lived in Brenda's undecorated house, with no Christmas at all. It made him shudder.

'When did *your* mum and dad get divorced?' Brenda asked.

William remembered those nasty things she'd said in school and decided it was about time she knew the truth.

'My parents aren't divorced,' William said. 'My mum died a long time ago.'

Brenda froze.

Her pale cheeks suddenly flushed red.

William guessed she was remembering what she'd said too.

'It's OK – you didn't know,' said William, and he scooped up a handful of snow, packed it into a neat ball and offered it to Brenda.

Brenda was too embarrassed to say anything, but sometimes the right words just don't exist anyway. She just stood there and cried again.

William caught a glimpse of the Christmasaurus's eyes peeking over the top of Brenda's wall. The dinosaur looked at Brenda, then back at William and gave a little nod with his head: *HUG!*

William screwed up his face. There was *NO WAY* he was going to give Brenda Payne a hug.

Nope.

No way.

Not a chance.

Then he looked at the girl in front of him, crying in the snow. The Christmasaurus snorted like a horse and frowned at William: *HUG!*

William rolled his eyes: *OK!*

BUMPING INTO BRENDA

He wheeled his chair a little closer to Brenda, who was now crying with her face in her hands. He looked at the dinosaur one last time and gave him a look that meant: *You'd better be right about this!* Then he took a deep breath, closed his eyes, leant forward with his arms wide open and gave the meanest girl in the school, possibly the world, a warm, friendly hug.

When he opened his eyes, he was shocked to find that Brenda was hugging him back.

Then suddenly they both dropped their arms and stared at the ground awkwardly.

'Don't you dare tell anyone about *that*!' said Brenda.

'Don't worry, I *definitely* won't!' replied William.

Then he saw the corners of Brenda's mouth rise up into a perfect little smile again.

'Thanks, though,' she said. 'I needed that.'

The Christmasaurus poked his head over and looked at William: *Told you so!*

CHAPTER TWENTY
SWAPPING SECRETS

'Why are you outside? Does your mum know you're out here?' asked William.

'Nope! She'd freak out if she caught me, but she's too busy avoiding Christmas to notice anyway,' Brenda explained. 'I just wanted to look at the other houses. They're so Christmassy. Besides, I'm in no rush to get back inside tonight. There won't be any presents waiting for me.' She sniffed.

'Why not?' said William. 'What about that plan of yours, at the postbox?'

'Oh, yeah. *That*,' Brenda said, kicking at the snow sheepishly. William could see she was remembering how she'd secretly edited innocent Nice List kids' letters to Santa, adding her own address.

'Why did you do it?' asked William.

Brenda took a deep breath.

'I guess that between the way I've behaved since Dad left, and Mum turning into the actual, real-life Grinch, I just thought my chances of getting any Christmas presents were so slim that I had to do something about it. I'm not even sure I believe in Santa anyway – but, if he does exist, then he's not an idiot. He'd have spotted my plan a mile off!' Brenda sighed. 'I won't be getting anything tonight. He's definitely put me on that Naughty List this year.' Brenda sniffed hard again and swallowed the snot that had frozen up her nose from sitting in the cold for so long.

'Well, maybe . . . maybe it's not Santa that puts you on the Naughty List. Maybe you put yourself there . . .' said William.

Brenda instinctively tightened her fingers into a fist, ready to punch William in the nose. But that was the old Brenda.

'I suppose you're right. Well, you know all my secrets

now, William. I think it's time you told me yours!' she said, taking William by surprise.

'Secrets? I, er, don't have any secrets,' replied William, who suddenly realized that his biggest secret was sitting a few metres away on the other side of Brenda's gate.

'Oh, *really?*' said Brenda suspiciously. 'Then tell me this, *Mr Willypoos:* what are you doing wandering the streets alone in the middle of the night on Christmas Eve?'

William was stumped. What could he say? How could he escape without Brenda seeing the Christmasaurus?

'Erm . . . is it the middle of the night?' William said in his best fake shocked voice, pretending he'd lost track of time. 'Oh, well, we'd really better be going!'

'*We?* Who's *WE?*' asked Brenda, becoming more and more suspicious as William started backing away, wheeling himself in reverse out of Brenda's front garden.

'Wait . . . where are you going? What are you hiding?' she called after him, but as William wasn't watching where he was going he failed to see the tip of the Christmasaurus's scaly tail lying on the ground across the open gate.

RooooAAAAR!!!!

Swapping Secrets

There was a deafening dinosaur yelp as the wheels of William's chair rolled painfully over the Christmasaurus's tail.

Complete stunned silence filled the air.

Brenda took one look at the unbelievable creature in front of her. She tried to get to her feet, but . . .

WHACK!

She fainted into the snow.

When Brenda finally came to, a few minutes later, William was staring anxiously down at her. The Christmasaurus was licking the snow from her face. Brenda let out a scream.

'William! Isn't that . . . it's a . . . d . . . di–'

'A dinosaur!' William finished the word for her. Now that Brenda had seen it, he didn't think there was any reason to keep pretending. 'It was a Christmas present from Santa!' he added proudly.

Brenda couldn't believe her eyes. She looked at the dinosaur's beautiful snowflake pattern, his icy, blueish scales that seemed to reflect every bit of light like diamonds.

'He's unbelievable!' she said.

'I know,' agreed William.

'He won't . . . eat us, will he?' Brenda gulped.

'Don't be silly – he'd never hurt us. He's my friend!' said William, and the Christmasaurus raised his head with pride. 'And he's my secret, Brenda. No one can know about him!'

William looked at Brenda, and he could tell she saw in his eyes that he meant it. She took a look through the window at her mum, who was now flicking through hundreds of television channels trying to find something un-Christmassy to watch.

'Let's shake on it,' she said. 'You know my secret, and I know yours, and we'll never tell a soul.'

William took her hand and shook it hard. 'Never tell a soul,' he repeated, and that was that.

'Well, what sort of dinosaur is he?' questioned Brenda, who was still looking a little nervous about the dinosaur in her garden.

'He's a . . . Well, it's obvious, really. He's . . .' William realized that he didn't actually know the answer.

'You mean, you don't even know what sort of dinosaur you're hanging around with? I thought you were supposed to know everything about dinosaurs!' Brenda fired back.

'How did you know that I like dinosaurs?' asked William, who didn't think Brenda took any notice of him and his interests.

Brenda's cheeks went a bit red as she quickly looked at the floor. 'Oh, I think I heard someone at school say it once . . .'

William looked at the dinosaur in the garden and realized that Brenda had a point. Why couldn't he work out what sort of dinosaur this was?

That gave William an idea.

'I know exactly where I can find out what sort of dinosaur he is!' cried William. 'The museum!'

He spun his wheelchair round to face the Christmasaurus. 'Want to see some other dinosaurs?' he asked with a smile.

The Christmasaurus jumped to attention. He couldn't believe what he was hearing. *Other dinosaurs?* There were *more dinosaurs?* So he wasn't the only one after all! He quickly nodded, desperate to see these dinosaurs William was talking about.

'It's not far!' William said to his dinosaur friend, then he turned to Brenda. 'Do you want to come with us?'

But Brenda didn't say anything.

Her face went white.

She was staring straight into her front room at her mother . . . who was staring straight at the dinosaur in the garden.

Swapping Secrets

Suddenly, the face at the window disappeared, and moved towards the front door.

'Quickly, we need to hide him!' said Brenda as her mother's footsteps came stomping down the hallway, just the other side of the door.

The Christmasaurus jumped back, tripped over William and fell into Brenda's stack of perfect snowballs. He quickly jumped to his feet with a pile of powdery snow on his head.

William had an idea.

'Quickly, cover him in snow!' he hissed as the sound of Brenda's mum turning the key in the lock rattled behind them.

Brenda and William scooped up as much snow in their hands as they could and threw it over the snowflake-patterned scales of the dinosaur in the garden.

'Hold still, dinosaur!' William whispered frantically, patting down the snow.

Brenda quickly took off her scarf and wrapped it round the dinosaur's thick, snow-covered neck just as her mum opened the door.

'What's all this?' said a very un-merry voice from the doorway.

'H-hello, Mrs . . . I mean, Miss . . . Brenda's mum,' stuttered William nervously.

'It's Miss Payne. What are you doing in my garden? It's the middle of the night!' Miss Payne said sharply as she scanned the garden, looking for the unbelievable creature she'd seen through the window. 'I thought I saw –'

SWAPPING SECRETS

'William was just making a snowman, Mum, see?' said Brenda, gesturing towards the lumpy snow-covered dinosaur, who now looked like an extremely poorly made snowman.

Miss Payne stared intently at their so-called snowman, looking it up and down, and just as she opened her mouth to say something she stopped. Her eyes were staring straight into the dinosaur's ice blue eyes that were gleaming out mesmerizingly from the snow.

That's when William saw it. Brenda did too. That little reluctant smile in the corner of Miss Payne's mouth, just like Brenda's. William couldn't help but think that her cold heart had thawed, just a little.

'Well, that's enough of that,' Miss Payne snapped. 'Brenda, inside *now*.'

Brenda marched into her house and William heard her footsteps running up the stairs.

'And you . . .'

'It's William, Miss Payne.'

'Go home at once,' she ordered.

'Of course. Merry Christmas!' William said with a

smile. He wheeled himself out of Brenda's front gate into the street, giving the snowman a little wink on the way.

The second William heard Miss Payne close the front door, he turned back and waited for the Christmasaurus, who was already shaking off his snowy disguise.

'Phew! That was close!' William said as he looped the fairy lights and tinsel around the dinosaur's head again. 'Ready to see some dinosaurs?'

The Christmasaurus let out a quiet but excited roar.

'Willypoos!' a small voice called out.

William looked up to see Brenda sneakily calling down from her bedroom window.

'I owe you . . . BIG time!' she called down. 'If you ever need anything, you know where you can find me!' With that, Brenda closed her window and disappeared inside her un-Christmassy house.

William couldn't quite believe his ears. Becoming friends with Brenda Payne was certainly the last thing he ever thought would happen this Christmas. Then he remembered that he was sitting behind a REAL dinosaur, on their way to his favourite place in the world – and he couldn't help but think that this might just be the best Christmas ever.

CHAPTER TWENTY-ONE

THE HUNT BEGINS

T he Hunter woke up to the smell of steaming dog breath as Growler licked him with his dry, crusty tongue.

'Get away, you disgusting giant tick-bus!' he snapped as he wobbled to his feet and tried to make sense of what had just happened. First he recalled falling from the roof. Then he remembered –

'The *dinosaur*! He got away!' the Hunter gasped. 'No. No. No. Not fair. That's not fair at all. NO NO NO!' he whined, and kicked in the snow like a stroppy toddler. 'I want that dinosaur. I want its head. I want it hanging on my wall and I want it NOW!' he screamed.

THE HUNT BEGINS

The Hunter snatched up his rifle from the snowy bush and marched across the street to William's wonky little house. He had had enough. No more hiding. He was going to burst through the front door, march inside and . . .

The Hunter stopped. He was standing at William's gate, staring at a hole in the front door . . . a *dinosaur*-shaped hole in the front door.

Then he noticed something on the ground at his feet.

'Dinosaur tracks!' he gasped.

There were large, clear dinosaur footprints in the snow, heading off down the street. Running through them were the thin tyre tracks of William's wheelchair.

'Haha! I've got him now!' the Hunter scoffed as he bent down and picked up a lump of snow that had been squashed by the Christmasaurus. The Hunter poked out his horrible tongue and tasted it.

'Yes. Yes,' he said to himself, trying to decipher the distinct taste of the dinosaur's tracks. 'That pesky little bullet dodger was lucky this time. I *never* miss a shot! Next time he won't be so lucky. GROWLER!' he cried, and his dog stood to attention at his side. 'Find that dinosaur!'

The dog instantly set to work, sniffing back and forth along the footprints and tyre tracks. He found the scent and let out a howl of excitement.

The hunt had begun.

CHAPTER TWENTY-TWO
CRACKING THE CODE

William yanked hard on the fairy lights, and the Christmasaurus came to a halt. They had stopped at the entrance to a magnificent building, with columns that extended from the snowy pavement to the sky above and an enormous archway overhead that was covered with intricate carvings of angels, animals, plants and people. The museum! The Christmasaurus thought it looked so wonderful that it would feel right at home in the North Pole.

'Pretty cool, right?' William said. 'One problem, though. We're not exactly visiting during opening hours . . .'

THE CHRISTMASAURUS

William pointed to the enormously grand doors that were very obviously locked shut behind a large sign that said *CLOSED UNTIL NEW YEAR*.

The Christmasaurus sighed and dipped his head in disappointment.

CRACKING THE CODE

'Not to worry, though,' William said with a mischievous grin. 'I know a secret way inside!' He pointed towards a small, shadowy archway that overhung a black, metallic-looking door, barely visible from the road.

THE CHRISTMASAURUS

The Christmasaurus tilted his head and his tail started wagging like an excited puppy. He'd never felt so excited before. He'd thought he'd never get to see *other* dinosaurs! He ran over towards this secret door in the shadows, dragging William's chair behind him, but he was suddenly stopped short.

Stairs!

The small, secret door sat at the top of a large, icy flight of stairs. He may not have been the smartest dinosaur, but he knew that there was no way William's chair could make it up a flight of stairs.

'In the daytime I use the wheelchair ramp,' William said. 'But that only goes to the main entrance, not this door.'

William hadn't thought about this. Maybe they wouldn't be going to the museum tonight after all. But the Christmasaurus wasn't going to let a few measly steps get in the way of him meeting other dinosaurs! He turned to William, lay down on the ground next to his wheelchair and let out a little grunt. William knew exactly what the dinosaur was saying. *GET ON!*

William didn't need any encouragement. He

scrambled excitedly out of his chair, using all his strength to heave his legs over the dinosaur's back, and with a little nudge here and there from the Christmasaurus he was finally sitting on top of his smooth, scaly back. He untangled most of the fairy lights from the dinosaur's neck until they were detached from the wheelchair.

'This is *much* better,' said William as the Christmasaurus stood and headed up the stairs towards the secret door. 'I wish I could ride you to school!'

When they reached the top of the steps and arrived at the shadowy door, the Christmasaurus gave it a nudge, but it was locked.

'We need to type in the security code,' said William, pointing to a small security box next to the door covered in numbers and flashing lights. The Christmasaurus had never seen such a weird contraption before. They had no security boxes or codes in the North Pole – it was protected by magic.

'Luckily, I just happen to know how to work out the code!' William said proudly. 'It's quite simple, really. I've seen it in a movie! It's so cold out tonight that the little number box is almost completely frozen, see?' William pointed at the little box. 'All the numbered buttons are covered in frost. All except for three of them.'

The Christmasaurus sniffed and studied the frosty numbered box, but it looked awfully confusing to his dino brain.

'You see, these three numbers don't have ice on them because these three have been pressed lots and lots today, so the ice has melted from them,' William explained, 'which means the security code *must* use these three numbers!'

The Christmasaurus looked closely and he could see

that William was right. All the buttons were frosted over except for three of them!

'So all we need to do is work out the correct order of these three numbers!' William exclaimed. 'Let's see: the unfrozen numbers are *ONE, TWO* and *FOUR.* I guess we should start at the beginning.'

He reached out his hand (which was now shaking with cold as he was only wearing his dinosaur PJs and a thin dressing gown) and he pressed the number *ONE.*

BLEEP!

A little red light flashed.

'Darn it! A red light means wrong!' William told the Christmasaurus. 'OK, so we know it doesn't start with number one!'

He reached out his freezing finger and pressed the number *TWO.*

BLEEP BLEEP!

This time a little green light flashed.

'YES! That means it was the right number, so the

code starts with the number two!' William's insides were all fluttery with excitement. He reached out again and pressed the next number. 'OK . . . number *FOUR*!'

BLEEP!

But another red light flashed. *Incorrect!*

Hmmmm, William thought to himself, then started the code from the beginning, with number *TWO*.

BLEEP BLEEP!

Green light!

There was only one other un-frosted button, number *ONE*. It had to be correct. He reached out and pushed it and waited for a green light, but . . .

BLEEP!

Red light. *Incorrect!*

He slumped down heavily on the dinosaur's shoulders, it all looked so hopeless all of a sudden.

'Oh, I'm sorry,' William said. 'I don't think I can work out the code. It's useless! What a rotten way to spend Christmas Eve.'

In the distance, a loud **CLONG!** echoed through the streets. It came from the clock tower as it chimed one o'clock in the morning.

'Well, I was wrong – it's not Christmas Eve any more. It's Christmas Day! What a rotten way to start Christmas Day . . . Wait just a second!' William had a thought. 'Yesterday was Christmas Eve, the *twenty-fourth* of December. *TWO* and *FOUR* are two of the unfrozen numbers in the code . . . but that was *yesterday*.' William's brain was ticking faster than the clock tower, and it suddenly ticked up an idea!

'What if . . .' he wondered, leaning in for one last crack at the code. 'What if the security code is the day's date?'

He quickly punched in the first number of the date: *TWO*.

BLEEP BLEEP!

The little green light twinkled.

'Which means that, at midnight, the code changed, making one of these un-frozen numbers *wrong* . . .'

He reached out and pushed a new number, the frosted number *FIVE*.

233

BLEEP BLEEP!

The green light twinkled again. Maybe William was right! With a shaky finger he punched in the next number.

ONE . . .

BLEEP BLEEP!

The twinkly green light lit up William's excited face as he pushed the final number.

TWO . . .

BLEEP BLEEP BLEEP . . . CLICK!

The lock flicked open.

'IT WORKED!' cried William. 'TWO, FIVE, ONE, TWO . . . The *twenty-fifth* of the *twelfth* . . . today's date! Merry Christmas!'

He punched the air in victory as the Christmasaurus nudged the door open with his nose and they stepped inside the museum.

234

CHAPTER TWENTY-THREE
ANCIENT GHOSTS

William's night was getting more and more bonkers. First Santa had brought him a *real* dinosaur for Christmas, and now he was riding on that dinosaur's back through the deserted museum in the middle of the night. What an adventure!

William steered the Christmasaurus out into the main hall, an enormous, gigantic, massively impressive room with something wonderful in the centre. It was a huge skeleton of a great diplodocus that was taller than a tree and as long as a train! It was one of William's favourite things in the museum.

The Christmasaurus couldn't believe his eyes. He'd never seen anything so huge in all his life!

Is this what other dinosaurs were like? he thought.

He walked closer to the towering dinosaur skeleton and saw that on one side there was a display with pictures and drawings of what this dinosaur would have looked like when it was alive, where it would have lived. It looked so green and hot there – nothing like where the Christmasaurus lived.

It was dark after hours in the museum. All the lights that usually illuminated the displays and exhibits were switched off, and the only light came from the street lights outside, which trickled in through high stained-glass windows in streaks of jagged colour. The effect was beautiful, but a little scary as it fell on the lifeless faces of all the weird and wonderful creatures on display, casting long, distorted shadows of the skeletons across the marbled floor.

William had never felt scared here before, but he was now. He was glad he wasn't alone!

As he clung tightly to the Christmasaurus's back, the dinosaur's footsteps echoed around the halls. The echoes

seemed to travel for miles through every hallway, every stairwell, bouncing off the ceiling and back to their ears so that even when they stopped moving it sounded as if someone were still walking behind them.

William kept checking over his shoulder nervously. Surely there was some sort of security guard at the museum somewhere, walking around checking on the place. Were the footsteps he could hear the echoed, ghost footsteps of the Christmasaurus, or was someone else in the museum?

And now William had the word *ghost* in his head! If there was one place he'd always thought must be haunted, it was the museum. It was full of ancient artefacts from around the world. Caskets of dead, mummified Egyptian pharaohs that had been dug up from their tombs. Hundreds of real, dead animals on display, from birds and fish to giant ship-sinking squid from the deep dark oceans, and jars full of real animal eyeballs and millions of insects in glass display cases. They were all deader than dead, but their ancient ghosts had to hang around somewhere, right?

It gave William the shudders, and the Christmasaurus

must have noticed it too, as he'd started walking on his tiptoes.

'Walk *that* way . . .' William whispered into the dinosaur's ear. They crept along the corridor until they reached a large set of heavy wooden doors. The sign above them said **DINOSAURS!**

'Right, let's see what sort of dinosaur *you* are!' William said, and the Christmasaurus pushed the doors open with his head. Once they were inside, William closed the doors behind them. That made him feel a bit safer!

This room was packed full of dinosaurs. There were dinosaur bones, dinosaur fossils, dinosaur skeletons, dinosaur paintings, dinosaur facts printed on the walls, dinosaur footprints moulded into the concrete floor. There was dino stuff everywhere! The Christmasaurus tried to take it all in as tears filled his icy blue eyes. William gave him a comforting rub on his head. These weren't the sort of *other* dinosaurs the Christmasaurus had been hoping for, but they were still amazing.

The first dinosaur they saw was a large, round, robotic model of a triceratops. As they stepped closer, it automatically switched on, let out a fake, digital-sounding *roar!* and bobbed its head up and down repeatedly. It had three pointy horns on its head.

'Nope! You're definitely not a triceratops,' William said, and they moved on to the next exhibit.

'Hmmmm, a T-rex . . .' said William thoughtfully, as they approached a tall skeleton of the mighty *Tyrannosaurus rex*. Its sharp, razor-like teeth grinned down at them. Even its lifeless skeleton was a frightening sight. 'No, I don't think you're related!' said William. 'Too scary!'

The Christmasaurus agreed. He wouldn't like to meet *that* dinosaur!

They moved on to the other displays in their search for one that might be the same as the Christmasaurus.

There was a spiny stegosaurus . . .

The Christmasaurus shook his head.

'Nope!' William cried.

A vicious velociraptor . . .

The Christmasaurus huffed and grunted.

'Definitely not!' agreed William.

A breathtaking brachiosaurus . . .

The Christmasaurus stood
on his tippy-claws and sighed.

'No, I don't think so either,' said William.

And so the search continued, but it began to seem hopeless. 'I can't seem to find any other dinosaurs like you anywhere!' William said, puzzled. 'What on earth could you be?'

Just then, the Christmasaurus saw something over his head that made his heart beat so hard it felt as if it were doing cartwheels in his chest (which I suppose would be called heartwheels!). William looked up and saw that the Christmasaurus was gawping at a wonderful winged dinosaur hanging from the ceiling as though it were gracefully flying.

'That's a pterodactyl,' William said. 'They were flying dinosaurs!'

The Christmasaurus went all giddy and wobbly, spinning around and jumping up and down excitedly so that William almost slipped off his back. There, hanging over the Christmasaurus's head, was proof that a dinosaur could fly!

'Whoa! Calm down!' William cried. '*They* could fly because they had wings!'

The Christmasaurus looked up and saw the pterodactyl's large wings stretching out on either side of its body.

'Only animals with wings can fly,' explained William.

But the Christmasaurus knew that wasn't true. He knew eight animals that didn't have wings, and he'd seen them flying earlier that very night: the reindeer!

Suddenly, a strange noise broke the silence of the museum.

'Ho, ho, ho! Merry Christmas!' a deep, jolly voice called out.

Santa!

The Christmasaurus bolted in the direction of Santa's voice. Was he really there at the museum? *Could it be?*

The sound led them to the room next to the dino hall:

the museum gift shop. The whole shop was covered from top to bottom in Christmas decorations of all sorts. Tinsel, bells, icicles, baubles: you name it, they had it. But what do you expect? This *was* where Mr Trundle worked, after all!

As they stepped inside, they saw a small plastic Santa, littler than an elf, positioned on the gemstone and fossil counter. Every few minutes, the tiny fake Santa would robotically wave his hand and chime one of a selection of recorded Christmas messages.

The Christmasaurus dropped his head in disappointment. First it was fake dinosaurs, now fake Santas! But then he saw something that gave him an idea.

Right in the centre of the shop was a large display of Christmas cards for sale. He quickly trotted over and searched the rows of festive cards.

'What are you looking for?' asked William, completely befuddled by what the dinosaur was doing.

The Christmasaurus suddenly wagged his tail. He'd found what he was after!

He gently slurped up a Christmas card using

his slobbery tongue and the card stuck to it like a postage stamp. He hurried back into the room full of dinosaurs and waddled around to the sign that said STEGOSAURUS. He started chewing and nibbling on the Christmas card in his mouth, dropping bits of cardboard on the floor. Then, when he was done, the dinosaur carefully used his tongue to stick the remaining bit of card over the sign. He stepped back so that William could see that it now said

'*CHRISTMASAURUS*,' William read. 'You're a Christmasaurus?'

The dinosaur wriggled excitedly beneath him and did a little jog on the spot.

'Wow! I've never even heard of a Christmasaurus before! Are there more of you?' William asked.

The Christmasaurus stopped his happy jog instantly and shook his head sadly.

'You're the only one?'

The Christmasaurus nodded.

'The One and Only Christmasaurus!' William exclaimed, stretching his arms triumphantly as his voice echoed around the hall, sounding far more epic than sad.

The Christmasaurus suddenly felt happier. Maybe being one of a kind wasn't a bad thing after all! He looked around him at all the bones and skeletons, then noticed something on the wall behind them. It was a huge mural of a vast jungle landscape. The painted sky was ferocious, with flaming rocks streaking across it. It didn't look like a nice place to live.

'That's where you're from,' explained William, but the Christmasaurus shook his head immediately. This wasn't where he was from at all. This dry-looking, fiery place was not his home! He quickly carried William back out of the dinosaur hall into the Christmassy gift shop again, where there were dozens of Christmas cards and Christmas gifts with pictures and drawings depicting the North Pole. Although none of them were exactly right, they were closer to the Christmasaurus's home than that terrifying mural in the other room!

The Christmasaurus picked up a mouthful of cards with images of the North Pole, the Northern Lights, Santa and some flying reindeer, and he dropped them all on the floor in front of him so that William could see the selection. William looked over the Christmasaurus's shoulder at the images and he could see from the glimmer of love in the Christmasaurus's eyes that he was looking at his home.

'That's where you're from? The North Pole?' William asked.

The Christmasaurus nodded with a deflated sigh.

William was starting to think that perhaps this dinosaur wasn't meant for him after all. Perhaps there had been some mistake. He started to wonder if maybe the Christmasaurus was lost.

'I think we'd better get back home,' said William as

CLONG! CLONG!

rang out from the clock tower outside. They had been in the museum for an hour.

The Christmasaurus headed through the giant entrance hall, past the colossal diplodocus and out of the door through which they had entered. He carefully walked William down the steps towards his waiting wheelchair, which now had a light dusting of snow on the seat. As they got closer, William noticed something. There was something rather large sticking out from underneath his wheelchair. Something big and spotty was caught in the under-seat basket in which William usually carried his school books.

'What on earth is this?' he asked as he lowered himself slowly from the dinosaur's shoulders back into his chair. He reached round and gave a pull on whatever it was that was stuck. It took a few hard tugs before it came free, but eventually he found himself sitting with a large, crumpled present on his lap.

'Ah! My Christmas present! I saw this sitting on my bed just before . . .'

He stopped for a second. He was having a moment of realization. William quickly unwrapped the present on his lap and saw two piercing golden eyes looking into his own.

He gasped. It was the most incredible toy dinosaur he had ever seen. William ran his fingers along the faultless red stitching and felt the smooth snowflake-patterned surface of its skin. He held it out in front of him and saw that it was almost a perfect replica of the Christmasaurus. It completely took his breath away!

The Christmasaurus hopped on the spot with excitement. He nudged the toy towards William, and William understood. The stuffed dinosaur was for him.

'Santa didn't bring me a *real* dinosaur for Christmas, did he? This toy is my present. Which means that you . . .' He stopped as the Christmasaurus looked to the sky and let out a howl-like roar at another plane flying overhead. 'You must be lost!'

Suddenly something very strange happened. The hairs on William's arms and the back of his neck all stood on end. It was very cold, but it wasn't the temperature that had caused them to stand on end. It was because he felt as if he were being watched.

Then, out of nowhere, a waft of something sickly and bitter drifted through the air and found its way to William's nose. It was a horrid smell. It smelt like smoke.

Pipe smoke!

The Hunter was close.

Chapter Twenty-four
FLIGHT AT THE MUSEUM

A bullet suddenly whizzed past, millimetres away from William and the Christmasaurus. It smashed the street light behind them, sending shards of glass showering down on to the street below.

'That was a warning shot!' screeched a villainous voice from somewhere at the far end of the street. 'Now wheel yourself away from that dinosaur, you little lump of pointlessness – unless you want to join him on my wall. I'm sure I can make room for a little head like yours!'

William had no idea what to do. His heart was doing all different sorts of heartwheels. His brain was racing at a million miles an hour. The vision he'd had earlier of *The Best Christmas Ever* definitely didn't involve a maniac with a gun!

He thought fast, then pushed Stuffy back into the wrapping paper, shoved it under the seat of his wheelchair, looped the fairy lights round the dinosaur's head and screamed, 'RUN!'

The Christmasaurus burst into action instantly. He may have been pulling a boy in a wheelchair and a stuffed dinosaur, but he was still fast!

'Stop! Stop! Stop!' cried the Hunter as he saw his prize racing away. Gunshots suddenly cut through the air – **BANG! BANG!** – slicing snowflakes clean in half, but they missed the Christmasaurus and William. *They* were too fast!

Flight at the Museum

'Growler. Fetch!' the Hunter commanded, and his trusty companion zoomed down the street after them.

'Faster, Christmasaurus, faster!' William cried, holding on for dear life, ducking and dodging the Hunter's shots. Crouched low in his chair, William couldn't see where the Christmasaurus was going. He could only feel him twisting and turning as he dashed between parked cars and whizzed along the street at the side of the museum.

The street at the side of the museum . . . William suddenly had an awful realization!

'It's a DEAD END!' he screamed as the Christmasaurus dug his claws into the snow and skidded to a halt, stopping just before they slammed into a brick wall.

They were trapped.

They waited, trembling, at the end of the long, straight, dead-end street. The large museum towered over them on one side and a row of locked offices loomed on the other. The only way out was the way they had entered and Growler was just prowling round the corner, baring his sharp, hungry teeth, cutting off their only chance of escape!

A few moments later the Hunter caught up. He appeared in the distance with his rifle raised and aimed it at the Christmasaurus and William.

'Good dog, Growler,' he said, and he dropped him a scrap of raw meat from his pocket as a reward. 'Game over, little boy. You're trapped. HA! You'd have to fly to get out of this one!'

William suddenly caught the Christmasaurus's eye and saw that there was a twinkle in it that he hadn't seen before. As if he had changed somehow. The Christmasaurus looked back at William, and William knew exactly what he was thinking.

'*That's it!*' he whispered. 'You have to *fly*!'

William heard his father's voice in his head. '*Believing is seeing,*' Mr Trundle had explained. He looked the Christmasaurus square in the eyes. 'I know you can do it!' he said. 'I never would have believed that a dinosaur existed, but here you are. I never would have believed that a *real* dinosaur would be my friend, but here you are! There are so many things that I never would have believed before tonight, so many seemingly impossible things that might just actually be possible – you just need to believe. Well, guess what, Christmasaurus? I *believe* that you can fly!' said William, completely honestly. 'I believe in you!'

As those words left his lips, something incredible happened. All the fairy lights that were wrapped around the Christmasaurus and William's wheelchair lit up! They glowed brighter and stronger than William had ever seen.

The Christmasaurus felt it too. Something had just changed in him as he stood wrapped in the glow of a hundred twinkly lights. He knew he could do it. He didn't just *want* to fly. He *believed* he could fly!

The Christmasaurus suddenly burst into the fastest run he'd ever managed before, pulling William behind him with the gleaming reins of dazzling fairy lights, and heading straight for the Hunter.

'What – the – devil?' spat the Hunter. 'Stop, this instant!'

But they didn't stop. They kept going, faster and faster.

'I'm going to count to three, and then it's over for you and your dinosaur, *boy*!' the Hunter called out, but the Christmasaurus didn't slow down. 'ONE!' he shouted.

The Christmasaurus gained speed.

'You can do it!' William cried.

'TWO!' the Hunter screamed, tightening his grip on his rifle.

The Christmasaurus took longer strides, getting a little higher with each step.

'THREE!' yelled the Hunter, and he closed one eye and aimed down the sight of his rifle, just in time to see the Christmasaurus take one final, giant, almighty leap into the air . . .

FLIGHT AT THE MUSEUM

He was flying.

The Christmasaurus was FLYING!

The Hunter and his dog were standing directly under the flight path of the flying dinosaur as he pulled William's chair into the air behind him. They dived for cover, William's wheels skimming the tip of the peacock feather in the Hunter's hat, the Hunter dropping his rifle in shock.

'A f-f-f-*flying* dinosaur?' the Hunter stuttered in amazement as he watched the Christmasaurus and William soar higher into the air, whizzing along the street. 'A FLYING dinosaur? I MUST HAVE ITS HEAD!' he howled like a madman into the sky.

William grabbed hold of the luminous reins and steered the flying Christmasaurus up and round the grand exterior of the museum. From the air the building looked even more amazing. In fact, everything suddenly looked more amazing. The snowy streets of William's town, the clock tower in the distance, the white rooftops – it all looked magical all of a sudden. But then William realized the most magical sight of all was directly in front of him, pulling his wheelchair like a sleigh across the Christmas sky. A flying dinosaur!

CHAPTER TWENTY-FIVE

THE CANDY CANE

William and the Christmasaurus flew higher and higher into the sky. It was the most glorious feeling either of them had ever felt. It was, hands down, head and shoulders, unquestionably, without doubt, the best, most awesomely cool night of both their lives . . . by miles!

There had been so much excitement and commotion that William suddenly felt completely exhausted. His power-bar had hit zero: batteries drained. He was safe now, flying behind the Christmasaurus, and the warm, magical feeling inside him made him feel so sleepy.

Before he knew it, he was snoring away happily twenty thousand feet in the air whilst the Christmasaurus flew on into the night.

William woke up suddenly as a blast of bright light exploded out of nowhere. How long had he been asleep? It only felt like minutes! He looked over the side of his wheelchair and saw that they were no longer flying over the streets and houses of William's town at the edge of the city. They were over pure, white, snowy mountains. He must have been asleep for hours! As the fresh, snowy air chilled his cheeks William tucked his hands inside the sleeves of his thin dressing gown, wishing he were wearing a little more than his dinosaur pyjamas!

FLASH!

There it was again. A vibrant explosion of greeny-blue light illuminated the entire sky.

The Northern Lights!

The Christmasaurus let out a happy roar of excitement. He was almost home. He suddenly started climbing, steeper and steeper until they were completely vertical, facing the moon!

'*Whaaaat . . . aaaaare . . . yooooou . . . doooooing?*' William cried, clinging on for dear life as the Christmasaurus kept flying up and up. Lucky William had had that seatbelt installed in his chair! He quickly tightened the buckle just in time, as the Christmasaurus flew an enormous loop-the-loop through the dancing Northern Lights. As scared as William was, he couldn't help but give into temptation and whilst he was upside down he reached out his hand and dipped it into the wonderful dancing colours in the sky. It didn't feel like anything he'd ever felt before. It wasn't like light; it was like running your hand through warm, melted butter.

William's dinosaur pilot performed some more daring aerobatics – loopy twists and twisty loops – and when they were finally back up the right way William was a little sick over the side of his chair (unbeknown to him, it had landed on an elf's roof below!).

The Christmasaurus made a little scoffing sound.

'It's not funny!' William said, nearly throwing up again as the Christmasaurus started descending on the gigantic mountains below. He weaved gracefully in and out of cracks in the cliffs until the mountains cleared in front of them and all William could see was an infinite sea of pure white snow.

The Christmasaurus landed with a little bump, which, for his first landing, wasn't a bad effort. Years of watching the reindeer had definitely paid off! They came to a sudden stop in the middle of the stark white nothing. William looked around him and saw absolutely zilch! He did a 360° scan and confirmed that they had flown all the way to nowhere!

But for some strange reason the Christmasaurus looked wonderfully happy! He was jumping up and down, wagging his tail like a puppy, letting out all sorts of strange roars that William hadn't heard before. He certainly didn't seem to be lost. In fact, the Christmasaurus seemed to be exactly where he wanted to be!

'Erm . . . excuse me, Christmasaurus, but . . . where are we?' William asked.

The dinosaur suddenly stopped. He looked at William as if he had gone completely barmy. He roared a little chirpy roar, wiggled his head around and gestured for William to open his eyes, as if he were missing something incredibly obvious!

'There's *nothing* here,' said William truthfully. He couldn't see anything at all.

The Christmasaurus shook his head with utter bewilderment, as though William had said something absolutely potty.

As William watched, the dinosaur suddenly seemed to become all flustered and frustrated, and tried to wriggle himself free from the fairy lights that were tangled around his body. William wheeled closer and helped unloop the things he'd been using as reins all night. But just as he pulled the very last loop of lights over the Christmasaurus's head, something unthinkable happened.

POP!

The Christmasaurus disappeared!

Just like that.

In the wink of a blink of an eye.

One moment he was right there, a few millimetres from William's face. The next he was gone! William looked around. Was this some kind of trick?

'Hello?' he called, but his voice drifted on the frozen wind into the distant nothingness. There was only snow as far as his eyes could see. He was sitting in his wheelchair, holding the string of unlit fairy lights, suddenly feeling very lonely and just a little bit scared.

All of a sudden, a gust of wind whooshed past and

THE CANDY CANE

William thought he heard whispers. He couldn't make out exactly what they said, though – it was more noises than words.

'Is anyone there? Christmasaurus?' he called.

The breeze blew past again and he heard the same whispers. He quickly searched all around. Weirdly, William no longer felt alone. Even though all he could see was emptiness for miles and miles, he suddenly felt as if he were being watched again!

POP!

William heard something. He used his hand to shield his eyes from the falling snow but still only saw long, empty fields of white all the way to the distant mountains. Then something caught his eye. There *was* something there after all. Something small, sticking out of the snow a few metres away from him.

He wheeled himself over and pulled out a shiny, delicious-looking, red-and-white candy cane from the snow. He was sure it hadn't been there before! He examined the yummy, sugary cane. It looked exactly like the sort of candy cane you might hang on your Christmas

tree, except it was perhaps just a tiny bit larger and heavier, and somehow more scrummy-looking. As he turned it around in his hands, he noticed something. On the flat, circular bottom of the cane there was very small but very neat writing, like the writing that runs through the centre of a stick of rock you sometimes get at the seaside. The tiny, perfect writing said: WILLIAM TRUNDLE.

William was stunned! How on earth was his name written in this oddly beautiful candy cane? Was he supposed to eat it?

William looked around at the forever emptiness and decided that he had nothing to lose. So he put the candy cane in his mouth and bit off a chunk.

POP!

As he bit down, the most spectacularly magical

thing happened. He didn't disappear like the Christmasaurus had. Quite the opposite, in fact: everything else *appeared*.

And by everything, I mean EVERYTHING!

Suddenly, William was sitting at the entrance to an enormous wooden building. It was the North Pole Snow Ranch. He couldn't believe how grand it was – its impressiveness reminded him of the museum! As he marvelled at the twisty turrets, the puffing chimneys, the toboggan-run path and the snowflake door knocker, his mouth dropped open with wonder. It was just like his dad's stories!

Then he noticed the animals, except they weren't animals – they were more like creatures. Magical creatures! There were small ones with wings whizzing overhead, trailing silvery dust behind them. There were snowmen in the distance, figure skating on a large frozen pool, performing fantastic swirls and twirls and occasionally pausing to pick up a carrot or piece of coal they'd lost in the process. Most of all he noticed the small, jittery little creatures that were now surrounding his wheelchair as the Christmasaurus happily greeted them with sloppy licks and tail swishes. Even though William had never seen one before, he

knew at once that these small creatures were elves!

'Hello, elves!' he said.

The elves all backed off and dived for cover, slightly scared of William. Then one by one they popped back out, looking frightened and cross, before all of a sudden they started singing!

'A child is here! A child, it's true!
Oh, what are we poor elves to do?
We could not leave him there to freeze –
He'd heard our whispers on the breeze –
And so we made a candy cane
Personalized with his name
So when that cane was licked and tasted
This boy was evaporated
Through the void of time and space
And brought here to this magic place.
We've never done what we just did.
Now what should we do with this kid?
He's seen our secret hiding spot –
Everything has gone to pot!
What will Santa think and say?
He'll be here soon; he's on the way!
He'll land here in that great red sleigh
And say, "Boy, you must go away!"
He'll be just as cross and grumpy
As he is fat and round and lumpy.
These things we say for you to hear,
But if you don't believe your ears

THE CANDY CANE

Then turn around, move out the way,
Santa's back, hip hip hooray!'

CHAPTER TWENTY-SIX
SANTA RETURNS

The elves stopped singing and stood back. William spun round to see a gigantic red sleigh appear out of thin air above them, and circle down very fast towards where he and the Christmasaurus were standing.

The sleigh was even more incredible than William could ever have dreamt it to be. Shimmeringly shiny, ridonkulously red and

monstrously
massive!

But that wasn't the most wonderful thing about it. The most wonderful thing, William thought, were the powerful creatures pulling it. He counted eight in total, striding through the air side by side. The flying reindeer. If he hadn't just spent the past few hours with a flying dinosaur, he would have said that these were the most amazing creatures he'd ever seen. Now he put them a very close second, behind the Christmasaurus!

'Whoa, whoa, whoa!' cried a deep, booming voice from overhead as the sleigh swooped round them and then touched down with a smooth *swish* along the snow. That's when William first saw him.

William couldn't believe his eyes. It was really him. Actually. Genuinely. One hundred per cent authentically.

The real deal.

'SANTA!' yelled William unexpectedly.

Santa pulled hard on the reins and the sleigh came to a stop directly in front of William, the Christmasaurus and the crowd of tiny elves that had gathered to greet him. The elves rushed forward, cheering and screaming like crazed fans at a rock concert, but William still had a perfect view of Santa as the elves were only half his height, even when sitting in his wheelchair!

The mind-blowingly massive man, dressed all in red, stepped down from his sleigh and for a moment looked every bit the jolly, happy, fat man you would expect him to be. But William was worried. The elf song had made him feel naughty, like he shouldn't be there! What would Santa do? What would he say?

272

William was about to find out.

'Hello, my elves! Merry Christmas! We've done it again, another year over!'

Then Santa spotted something out of place – William!

'What the crackers is *this*?' he asked, completely confuddled. He bounced straight towards William, who was squished in the centre of a crowd of elves, and stood, towering impressively, over him. 'You're a little tall for an elf! *Why*, you're not an elf at all! Nor snowman, or forest fairy, or reindeer! Tell me, are you a mountain troll? Yes, I've heard of lost, wandering trolls before, but never seen one. How fascinating!' He rubbed his hands together excitedly. 'Well, Merry Christmas, troll friend! Join us and we shall celebrate the season. *Ho ho ho!*'

'B-b-but . . . Mr Santa, s-s-sir . . .' William spluttered nervously. 'I'm not a troll!'

Santa paused and scratched his beard thoughtfully.

'No . . . of course you're not! Wait . . . don't tell me . . . you're a . . . bald yeti! *Yes!* That's it. How peculiar!'

'No!' William said. 'I'm not one of those either!'

'Hmmm, not a troll and not a bald yeti, eh? Don't tell me! I'm thinking, I'm thinking, I'm thinking . . .

Oh, what a fun guessing game this is! Isn't it fun, *ho-ho*!' and Santa did a little hop and a skip and walked around William, inspecting him.

As he circled the boy, the elves moved out of the way, revealing William's wheelchair.

'What's this? A one-man sleigh! How intriguing! I see no deer – what creature pulls your sleigh?'

'A flying dinosaur,' William said.

There was silence.

Everything was still.

'I'm sorry, my dear fellow, could you repeat yourself? I've had a very long night and my ears must be full of cloud, for I thought you said a *flying dinosaur*!'

'I did say that, Santa, sir!' William said politely. 'You see, I'm not a troll or a yeti. I'm just a boy!'

There was a sudden rumble of whispers and giggles from the surrounding elves.

'*Just* a boy?' Santa bellowed in his mighty jolly voice. William was unsure if he were jolly happy or jolly angry. '*JUST* a boy?' he repeated, and looked around at his elves. Then all of a sudden Santa seemed to find something completely hilarious.

'*Ha-HA-HA! Ho-HO HO!*' He boomed an enormous laugh that made his belly ripple and wobble. Then all the elves joined in the laughter too. They laughed in the most peculiar way. It was as if they'd been meticulously rehearsing the laugh for weeks with very complicated harmonies and rhythms. William thought it was fantastic. In fact, he thought it was very funny! Before he knew it, he felt a little chuckle rising up inside him too, and suddenly found himself laughing with them. And because William was laughing the Christmasaurus thought he should probably join in.

So, there they all were: Santa, the elves, William and the Christmasaurus, with uncontrollable giggly laughs. They laughed and howled giggles and roars for so very long that by the time they had calmed down William had forgotten what they were laughing at.

'*Oh*, Santa! . . . What . . . on earth was so funny? I can't remember!' William asked, wiping the tears away from his chilly cheeks.

'Well, I was laughing because you said you were *JUST* a boy!' Santa said, still finding the thought amusing.

'But I *am*,' said William. 'I am *just* a boy!'

'My dear confused little friend, you can't be! There's no such thing as JUST a boy.'

William was awfully confused.

'Allow me to explain,' Santa said. 'You see, up here we have all sorts of wonderfully magical creatures. Flying reindeer. Skating snowmen. Forest fairies. And lots more! But there's something we don't have, we, the most magical creatures in all the world . . .'

William didn't have a clue what that could be.

'Children!' Santa said with a smile.

'*Children?*' William said. 'Children aren't magic. I'm a child and I'm not magic at all!'

All the elves giggled and Santa smiled knowingly.

'Oh, but you are! You really, truly are. You just don't know it! You can create impossible worlds in your imagination that don't really exist. *That* is magic. Because you can only see the best in people, the best in the world, in life. *That* is magic. Because you understand the importance of silliness, the importance of fun, of laughing and playing, which grown-ups have forgotten. *That* is magic. But, most of all, because you believe, without question, in the impossible. Without needing

proof. Without hesitation. *That* is magic.'

William couldn't believe what he was hearing. He could do all of those things and he hadn't even realized that they were magic!

Santa nodded and continued. 'That is the reason I am able to exist . . . *William Trundle.*'

At the mention of his full name, William couldn't help but notice that all the elves started whispering among themselves.

Santa gave them a big jolly smile with his wise eyes and they calmed down.

'How do you know my name?' William asked.

'Well, it took me a moment to realize. I didn't expect to see a boy here in the North Pole. We haven't had a boy here for a very long time,' said Santa thoughtfully. 'But, once I knew that you really were a boy, it was obvious. There was only one boy *you* could be.' Santa reached into his pocket, pulled out a piece of paper and handed it to William.

'My letter!' said William, recognizing it at once.

'Yes. It gave me quite some trouble, this one!' Santa said, handing the letter to William. William started reading his handwriting, as Santa recited the words from memory.

'*Dear Santa, for Christmas this year I would like a lot of things that you probably can't give me, but a* **dinosaur** *would make me very happy! Merry Christmas . . . William Trundle.*'

Santa looked down at William as though he were trying to read his mind. 'Tell me, William, what are these *things* you speak of? For this is the North Pole. It's the place where dreams come true. More specifically, where *children's* dreams come true.'

William's heart skipped a thump.

'My dreams can come true here?' he asked.

'Absolutely. Dreams, wishes, hopes – you name it!' replied Santa confidently. 'This entire place is *made* from children's dreams! It is the one place in the entire world where whatever you truly desire can materialize before your very eyes.'

'But that can't be true,' said William causing all the elves to gasp again.

'And why do you think that, young William?' asked Santa, looking a little confused himself.

'Because if my dream, my wish, my true desire can come true here, then . . .'

William looked down thoughtfully at his wheelchair and wondered. Was it really possible if he truly wanted it? Then he took a deep breath and tried to do something . . . something impossible.

He tried to stand up.

CHAPTER TWENTY-SEVEN

WHAT WILLIAM REALLY WANTS

All the elves watched with amazement. Smaller elves climbed on taller elves' shoulders, who were already standing on the tallest elves to get a better view.

William wobbled a little as his hands gripped the armrests of his wheelchair. He scrunched his face up tight and held his breath. He tried to stand harder than he'd ever tried to do anything before. But it was no use. He slumped back into his chair, defeated.

He couldn't do it.

'See!' William said, looking up into Santa's warm face. 'You said that my dreams can come true here, but if that's true then why can't I walk?'

The North Pole had never been so quiet.

No one's dreams had ever *not* come true here before.

Santa's eyes stared deep into William's. His kind face had a wise sort of knowing smile, as though he already had the answer to every question you could possibly think of before you'd even thought of it.

'My dear William. Perhaps . . . could it be possible, maybe, that what you're asking for isn't what you *truly* desire?' asked Santa in the kindest, deepest, wisest voice.

William looked at his legs and then at his wheelchair. He'd been sitting in it for longer than he could remember. It was all he'd ever known. But William realized that until Brenda had come along and knocked his confidence, he'd never once wished for anything else. Maybe Santa was right. Maybe this wasn't what he *really* wanted.

'William, close your eyes. I want to try something. Let's see if we can unravel this riddle of yours,' said Santa, kneeling down beside William and placing his huge, warm hand on William's shoulder. He began to whisper. 'Breathe deep, William. Let the North Pole air inside your mind. It will help us to find what your heart is searching for.'

William breathed in the cool air. It was fresh and sweet with the smell of something familiar: toasted crumpets. It made William think of his dad.

'Good, William. Now I want you to stop searching. Stop *trying* to find what you want, and imagine you already have it. Don't just imagine it. *See* it. *Hear* it. *Feel* it . . . *believe* it.'

Suddenly, glorious music filled the air. Santa's gramophone had burst to life on its own, playing a song no one had ever heard before. It was beautiful.

William opened his eyes and was shocked to see hundreds of elves, the Christmasaurus and Santa all staring up at something. Something above William's head.

He swivelled his chair round in the snow, and what he saw completely took his breath away.

It was his dad in the sky.

The greens and blues, purples and yellows of the Northern Lights had wondrously weaved into the

shape of Mr Trundle in the starry sky over the North Pole. William tried to take it all in. He realized he'd never seen his dad look so happy.

Then, all of a sudden, the lights and colours started swaying and swirling around to the sound pouring from the gramophone, and William realized his father wasn't alone in the sky.

Mr Trundle was dancing with a woman.

He lovingly spun her over the stars and they waltzed across the sky.

Tears filled William's eyes as the Northern Lights faded and the song slowed and softened.

'Family,' Santa whispered as William's vision in the sky came to an end. 'Your father's happiness. That is your *true* desire.'

All was quiet.

William was deep in thought. It was right there in the North Pole that he realized that he'd found what he truly wanted – and that walking wouldn't get him there. He stared down at his chair, but not in sadness this time. He was happy. Happy to be himself once again.

'Thank you, Santa,' William said with a smile. 'So . . . can I wish for a new girlfriend for my dad?'

'Oh, William, I'm very sorry, but I'm afraid I can't . . .' said Santa.

'But, Santa, think about it. That's a new girlfriend for Dad AND a new mum for me. We're basically sharing a present! Two birds with one stone!' said William with a cheeky sort of smile, still hoping it might be possible.

Santa chuckled to himself as he thoughtfully stroked

his beard. 'There are some things, William, that I simply can't do. There are rules to this job, you know.'

William listened closely as Santa explained.

'Firstly and most importantly: I can't make people die, and, believe me, you'd be surprised how many rotten eggs ask me to take out a teacher or two each year! Secondly and similarly: I can't make people come back to life. Thirdly and most frustratingly: I can't make cheesecakes. And lastly and most relevantly: *I can't make people fall in love.*'

William looked to the sky where he'd just seen his true desire, and sighed.

Noticing William's disappointment, Santa added, 'However, if there's one time of year that dramatically improves someone's chances of falling in love, then it's most certainly Christmastime. After all, it is the best time to fall in love.'

CHAPTER TWENTY-EIGHT
THE CHRISTMASAURUS STAYS

'Now, I think we should be taking you back to your father,' said Santa. 'It's Christmas morning, and I can't imagine he'll find any happiness in waking up to discover you've disappeared in the night!'

All of a sudden, William noticed that everything was starting to fade and go all fuzzy, like the world around him was ceasing to exist! He'd never fainted before, but he thought to himself that this might be what fainting would feel like. The magical place in which he was sitting was getting fainter and fainter, and suddenly he could see distant snowfields and mountains where the wonderful buildings had been.

'Quickly, William!' Santa's voice said from somewhere in the fading fuzz. 'Take a bite of the candy cane!'

William looked at the red-and-white treat with his name running through it that he'd forgotten he was holding. It was the only thing that hadn't seemed to fade out of existence. He looked back up to see nothing. Absolutely everything had gone. The sleigh. The reindeer. The elves. Everything had vanished!

'Hello?' he called out into the frozen emptiness.

He quickly popped the stick of candy into his mouth, and as he tasted its sweet deliciousness on his tongue the magical world reappeared before his eyes.

'What just happened?' asked William as Santa and the elves all revaporated in the same spot they were in just before.

'Well, William, lots of people would love to come to this place. Unfortunately, not all of those people are nice people. And we don't want horrid rotters turning up at the North Pole. No, no, no! So we protected it with magic,' Santa explained. 'You see, the North Pole is in another dimension. It's somewhere between Imagination and Make-Believe, but not quite as far as Unthinkable, and if you get to Not-Doable then you've definitely gone too far. To get here, you have to be invited, and to be invited you have to be good, truly good, through and through! When we have guests, if they're truly good, they are presented with one of these deliciously magical Cosmos Converting Candy Canes.'

Santa pointed to the half-eaten candy cane in William's hand. 'All they have to do is lick them, and they are filled with wonderful, tasty magic that allows them to see our world.'

'So what happens when they've eaten all the candy cane?' asked William curiously.

'Then their time here is up! Poof! Pop! GONE!' Santa said merrily. 'It's the only way anyone can get in or out! Quite a genius idea, actually. Thought of that one myself!'

William looked at what was left of the candy cane in his hand and suddenly wished it were a lot bigger, so that he could stay longer! Then he had a cheeky idea.

He quickly covered his Cosmos Converting Candy Cane with his hands and sneakily snapped off a small piece. He popped it up his pyjama sleeve, out of sight, then continued to suck on what was left in his hand. Now he had a way to get back here!

'That way we can keep the rotten, horridable stinkers out!' laughed Santa. 'Of course, it hasn't always been like this. There was a time when any old troubler could wander up here, willy-nilly.'

'Oh, Santa, that reminds me! There's something I need to tell you!' said William, who had almost forgotten about the evil Hunter.

William explained all about their night and the adventure they'd had. About how the hateful Hunter and his hideous hound had tried to shoot them and hang their heads on his wall. About how he had believed that the Christmasaurus could fly, and how he took off and flew all the way through the night to the North Pole.

'By golly gumdrops!' Santa said 'That does sound like an adventure! I'm afraid I know exactly the Hunter you're talking about. Bony fingers?'

'Yes!'

'Lumpy white scar down his face?'

'Yep!'

'Smokes a horrid, smelly pipe?'

'That's him! How do you know him?' asked William.

'Many Christmases ago, before the Hunter was the hunter, when he was still just a little boy named Huxley, he was very exceptionally naughty. Think of yourself on your naughtiest day, and I bet that's nowhere close to Huxley on his best behaviour! He was so naughty that I had no choice but to put him on the Naughty List, and I *hate* having to put children on the Naughty List,' Santa explained.

'As Huxley grew, so did his naughtiness. In fact, as time went on, he became well and truly rotten. He was vicious and cruel, and had discovered a rather horrible new hobby: he loved hunting animals. Even the family pets weren't safe when Huxley was around!'

Santa sat his huge bottom in the snow, getting himself comfortable for the next part of his story. William, the Christmasaurus and all the elves were gathered round, listening closely to every word Santa said. He was a great storyteller.

'One particular Christmas Eve, Huxley's little brother was awake far past his bedtime. He was peering out of his bedroom window, hoping to catch a glimpse of me, and, indeed, he saw my sleigh soaring overhead! Huxley cried out, and dashed to the window. That, I'm afraid, was the moment he saw my beautiful reindeer for the very first time. If only I had known, I would have taken a detour!

'As I was jollily plopping presents down the chimneys of the other children in their town, unbeknown to me, Huxley was hurriedly and horridly concocting a plan, and he did something unthinkably naughty – he persuaded his little brother to join him. As fast as they could, they scurried up the drainpipe and concealed themselves in the shadows of their rooftop before I arrived. When I landed on it, they sneakily, cheekily, crept into the back of my sleigh, keeping impossibly quiet. I was so full of Christmas jolliness, I totally missed them!' Santa said shaking his head.

'Huxley's mind was so rotten with greedy nastiness that when he got here, to this wonderfully magical place, he wanted it all. He wanted to take everything. Huxley, with his impressionable little brother following closely behind, snuck around the ranch, taking in all the wonderfully magical sights, smelling the wonderful smells. But there was already one thing on Huxley's mind. Something in particular that he wanted, that he truly desired!'

'What?' William cried. 'What did he want?'

'My Magnificently Magical Flying Reindeer,' Santa

said sadly, and he pointed to the incredible creatures still harnessed to the sleigh. 'They sneakily snuck their way to the stables, where Huxley made his brother climb on his shoulders and smash the window. He was small enough then to climb through and open the door for Huxley to step inside. That nasty little worm wasted no time. His greed and his hunting instincts clicked into overdrive as he leapt on to the back of one of my magnificent deer.'

All the elves gasped. Some even shrieked.

'He stole a flying reindeer?' William cried.

'Worse!' Santa said. 'Whilst clinging to the back of the frightened deer, Huxley pulled out a small golden pocket knife that he'd stolen from his wealthy father, and began to hack at the reindeer's antlers! But the deer wouldn't hold still. The deer launched high into the air inside the stables, smashing through the roof!'

Santa described it so well that it made William jump!

'His little brother, fearing for Huxley's life, grabbed hold of the deer's reins and tried to pull them back down, but the deer was too powerful for the young

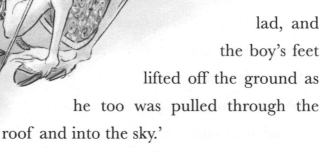

lad, and
the boy's feet
lifted off the ground as
he too was pulled through the
roof and into the sky.'

Santa paused and swallowed hard. William noticed that he was somehow not looking as jolly as he had, as though whatever he was about to say was really difficult.

'That's when things went from awfully dreadful to dreadfully awful. The young boy was so scared as he clung to the dangling reins in the sky that, in his panic, he began to wish the deer wouldn't fly.'

William felt his heart sink in his chest. He already knew what happened next.

'His wish came true?' William said.

Santa nodded.

'The deer came crashing down to the ground, with Huxley and his brother too. That was the last time that magnificent reindeer ever flew. When the young boy cleared the snow away from his eyes, he saw Huxley standing wickedly over the grounded deer, clutching a piece of its antler in his hateful hand. That's when I found them.'

'What did you do?' William asked.

'I had no choice, William, but to banish the boys from the North Pole. For ever,' Santa said, and all the elves burst into harmonious sobs.

'Of course, that little rotter Huxley quickly shoved the piece of antler into his brother's trembling hands in an attempt to pin the blame on him. That's when it happened. I couldn't help it! A huge, thick teardrop formed in the corner of my eye, and as it rolled down my cheek it froze and became a snowflake, floating through the air.'

The elves all paused in unison and took a breath before their tuneful sobbing continued.

'This snowflake was so full of my sadness that the very instant it landed on Huxley's shoulder, he disappeared from the North Pole.'

'He vanished?' said William.

'Banished!' replied Santa. 'My tears are the only thing strong enough to do it. Then I looked into the eyes of Huxley's little brother, who held out the piece of antler in his hand. 'You must keep it,' I told him, 'and let it remind you of what happened here tonight.' Then a second tear plopped out of my eye, froze on the air and banished the boy as he held the stolen antler to his heart.'

William thought Santa looked so sad that he might cry enough tears to banish him, the Christmasaurus, and every single one of the crowd of elves gathered around listening.

'What happened to them after they were banished?' said William curiously.

Santa looked into William's eyes again, and William got the funny feeling that Santa was thinking carefully about what he was saying.

'Well, Huxley became that repulsive, evil, maliciously rotten skinbag you met tonight. Unfortunately, seeing my magnificent deer up close only fuelled his obsession for rare animals and trophies. He's been trying to grabnab one of my flying reindeer every year since, but he never gets close to 'em.'

'Well, he got pretty close to *grabnabbing* a flying dinosaur tonight!' William said.

'That reminds me . . .' said Santa, and he turned and faced the Christmasaurus.

'My dear little dinosaur, what the jingle were you doing in this young boy's house?'

The Christmasaurus looked ashamed. He stood and walked round to the back of William's wheelchair and pulled something large out from underneath the seat with his mouth. It was Stuffy, its head peeking out of the wrapping paper.

'I don't believe my bogglers. You went all that way to get another look at this stuffed toy? You are a dongle-brained, wallychops dinosaur, aren't you! You could have been lost for ever! It's not safe for you down there,' said Santa. 'You have to stay here. *This* is your home!'

The Christmasaurus quickly shuffled over to William and parked his scaly bottom next to his wheelchair, wagging his tail hopefully at Santa.

'Oh, but, Santa, can't the Christmasaurus stay with me? I promise to look after him!' pleaded William. 'I'm not mean and awful like that Hunter!'

'I know you're not, William. You are a good, kind boy, with a kind, good heart, but there are some nasty people out there, William. Nasty people like the Hunter, who would love to grabnab themselves a Christmasaurus. Up here, with us, is the only place he is safe. The only place that evil rotter can't find him!'

'But I know all about dinosaurs, and dinosaurs don't come from the North Pole!' said William, desperate for the Christmasaurus to come home with him.

'He might not be *from* here, but he *belongs* here,' Santa said with a soft, wise smile.

William knew he was right. As he looked around at all the magical creatures staring at him – elves, fairies, snowmen, narwhals, polar bears (even the mountains themselves seemed to be alive) – he realized that *this* was the Christmasaurus's home. How could a flying dinosaur ever fit in anywhere other than the North Pole? It was the perfect place for him.

The Christmasaurus knew it too. He wished he could see William every day, but he loved the North Pole with all his heart and could never leave.

William and the Christmasaurus looked each other in the eye. The Christmasaurus let out a long sad huff and dipped his head to the ground. William hated goodbyes too.

Santa placed a hand on the Christmasaurus's head and the other on William's shoulder and whispered, 'A friend for Christmas is a friend for ever.'

Suddenly William felt as though the ground were moving. He looked down and saw that eight elves had picked up his wheelchair and were hoisting him towards the sleigh. It was Snozzletrump, Specklehump, Sparklefoot, Sugarsnout, Starlump, Spudcheeks, Snowcrumb and Sprout, and they were singing (of course!).

'We're sending William on his way
Back home again this Christmas Day.
He's seen a lot tonight for sure,

From flying Christmas dinosaurs
To evil hunters and their hounds,
Then somehow this boy William found
His way to this enchanted place
And from the look upon his face
He liked it – well of course he did:
It's all a dreamworld for a kid.
There's so much more to show you, BUT
Your time is done – you've seen enough.
Now get back home and don't delay!
Quick, hoist him up upon the sleigh!'

The elves finished singing and with a large *Heave-Ho!* lifted William in his chair into Santa's sleigh. Santa hopped to his feet and did some sort of cartwheel thingy and plonked his enormous bottom next to William. He really was an oddly jolly man!

Amongst the crowd of elves William saw the shimmering blue head of the Christmasaurus. As the dinosaur took a step towards him he could see that William was crying. His tears froze instantly on his cheeks and tiny, dusty snowflakes fell away.

THE CHRISTMASAURUS STAYS

'Goodbye, Christmasaurus,' William said, suddenly finding it difficult to speak. 'I'm so glad I met you . . .'

At that, the Christmasaurus bent his head down low and gave William a goodbye hug. William wished he didn't have to say goodbye, but he knew it was the right thing to do, and sometimes the right things to do are the hardest.

He wiped a tear away from his cheek as Santa wound up the old gramophone again. Glorious music lifted the sleigh from the floor as the elves and the Christmasaurus took a step back. Santa took a deep breath and was just about to sing when he looked at William and said, with a cheeky smile, 'You can join in if you know the words!'

And with that he burst into song, and the reindeer galloped excitedly into the warm Northern Lights once again. William couldn't believe his eyes or his ears. He was sitting in Santa's sleigh, flying into the night sky with Santa himself sitting next to him . . . singing!

He looked over the side of the sleigh and gave one final wave to his new dinosaur friend. Just before the magical effects of the candy cane wore off, he noticed a lone reindeer below, standing gracefully on the roof of the Snow

THE CHRISTMASAURUS STAYS

Ranch with a piece of its left antler missing. William watched as the reindeer clopped towards the grand chimney breast that puffed glittery smoke into the air.

It raised a golden glowing hoof and gently dipped it into the smoke, and at the slightest touch the golden glow spread like warm magic up through the clouds, transforming them from billows of smoke into thick shafts of coloured lights, dancing through the sky.

William watched as the wonderful world below faded into nothing, and wondered if perhaps that deer, too, had found its true desire in the Northern Lights. He hoped so.

Chapter Twenty-nine

SMOKE

Santa's eight reindeer pulled the sleigh through the sky much faster than the Christmasaurus had pulled William's wheelchair and so they found themselves flying over William's town in no time at all.

'That's my house, right there! The little wonky one!' cried William excitedly as he saw the warm glow of the morning sun turn all the snowy rooftops orange. Santa steered the deer down to William's rooftop and landed with no trouble at all.

'Wow, thanks!' William called to the eight wonderful deer.

'Right, let's get you inside!' Santa said as he backflipped down from the sleigh and picked up William and his wheelchair with one arm, no problem. He skipped over to the chimney and placed William in his chair frighteningly close to the edge.

'That's tiny! We'll never fit down there!' William exclaimed, staring at the teensy hole in the top of the chimney.

Santa said nothing, but smiled at William. Suddenly, William had the most bizarre sensation that he was shrinking. Or was everything else growing? Either way, in the blink of an eye, the tiny hole in the top of William's chimney flue was now an enormous hole, big enough for at least two Santas to fit down.

'I'd better go first,' said Santa. 'I wouldn't want to land on you!' And with that he did a large, double-twisty backflip into the darkness of the chimney. 'Follow meeeeee!'

Whoa! William thought. He stared down into the dark, black hole and suddenly wasn't so sure he had the courage to do it.

That's when everything started shrinking around

him. Or was he growing? Whatever it was, the hole in
the chimney was getting smaller! There was no time to
think. It was now or never. He closed his eyes, took a
deep breath and gave his wheels a big, hard push!

He fell down the chimney as fast as a rocket, spinning
wildly out of control. He could feel the walls tightening
around him as the chimney flue got smaller and smaller.
Then he saw something very large and very dark coming
towards him very, VERY fast!

William's wheels never touched the ground.

He was swooped out of the fireplace in some sort of thick, ropey net!

'GOTCHA!' he heard a voice cackle, as something awful and stinky stung his nostrils . . . . *PIPE SMOKE!*

It was the Hunter! He was there, in William's house! They'd jumped right into a trap!

William twisted and punched his fists through the holes in the net as the Hunter hoisted him into the air and hung him in the middle of the room from the ceiling fan.

SMOKE

'I KNEW IT! I told you, Growler, I told you they'd come back. What did I say? I said, *"There's no way they'll keep that little wheelchair boy up there in the North Pole. They'll bring him home, and when they do we'll be there waiting!"* That's what I said. AND I WAS RIGHT! HA!' the Hunter boasted in his wickedly posh voice, with thick, smelly smoke pouring from his nostrils like a dragon as he cackled.

William wriggled as hard as he could, but the ropes from the net held him tight in his chair, dangling from the ceiling fan. He stopped fighting for a moment as he swung helplessly and took a glance around his living room. As the room spun he caught a glimpse of an awfully, terribly, horrid sight. Santa was lying in a large heap on the floor below him with his hands tied tightly behind his back so that he couldn't move.

'Santa!' William cried.

'Silence, boy, or your daddy is done for!' spat the Hunter, standing with one foot triumphantly on Santa's back, his sniper rifle raised and aimed, ready to fire at any moment.

William looked to where it was pointing and saw the

most awful thing he'd seen yet. His dad was tied up with thick ropes in the corner of the room, staring back at William through cracked glasses with wide, terrified eyes. Growler was pacing back and forth, menacingly baring his teeth whenever Mr Trundle tried to speak.

William instinctively lashed out again, punching through the holes in the net, trying to reach the horrid Hunter.

SMOKE

'Now, listen to me, you stupid, puny little child. I'm going to speak slowly, so that your undersized brain can understand me, as I'm only going to say this once.' The Hunter looked William directly in the eye and William saw how wretchedly evil this man truly was. There was no chance he was ever returning to the Nice List!

'Where. Is. That. FLYING. Dinosaur?' he whispered in the most terrifying whisper William had ever heard.

'Don' 'ell 'im, 'illiam!' Santa mumbled, struggling to get his words out as he was lying face down with his mouth full of beard!

'Shut it, fattypants. I'll deal with you later!' barked the Hunter.

'LEAVE HIM ALONE!' screamed William.

Everything fell silent as he swung himself round so that he was facing the Hunter. William had had enough.

'You're just an evil, horrid, nasty, sick, twisted man, and that's why you'll never find the Christmasaurus.' Tears were streaming down William's face and dripping off his chin. 'He's in the safest, most magical place in the world now, and you'll never find it. You'll NEVER get back there!'

''Illiam! Don't say any . . . m-more!' Santa called, but William couldn't hear his muffled plea. He was crying and shouting with so much emotion that he just couldn't help the next thing he said from coming out of his mouth:

'You'll never find him because you're a rotten, stinking, trophy-hunting killer,' William screamed, 'and they'll *never* give you a Cosmos Converting Candy Cane!'

It was at that very moment, as he pointed his fist at the Hunter, that the small piece of his own magical candy cane that he'd secretly hidden flew out from his sleeve and hurtled through the air. It shimmered and sparkled magically as it spun in front of the Hunter's evil black eyes before landing with a delicate CLINK! at his feet.

The Hunter let out the most wicked, triumphant laugh, blowing stinky smoke from his pipe around the room as he swiped up the delicious-looking piece of magic candy from the floor.

'I have one now! That flying dinosaur's head is practically mine. Mine! ALL MINE!' he cackled and puffed, puffed and cackled as he danced around the room like a maniac, firing victory shots from his rifle into the Trundles' living-room ceiling, while waving the piece of magical red-and-white candy cane around like he'd won a golden ticket. He had a way to the North Pole. Nothing could stop him now!

Then all of a sudden, the Hunter heard a sound that made his heart stop. It came from out in the street.

RooooAAAAR!!!!

It was the unmistakable roar of a dinosaur.

The Christmasaurus was *here*!

CHAPTER THIRTY
A TRUNDLE TORNADO

he Hunter sprang out of the living room in a
flash, leaving only a thick cloud of smoke from
his pipe. Growler wasted no time hanging around
either, and followed him straight out of the door. The
hunt was on. Their prey was close!

'We've got him this time, Growler!' William heard
the Hunter cry as his voice disappeared out through the
front door and into the street.

The Christmasaurus was in danger! William *had* to get
free from the net and help him, but he felt more trapped
than he'd ever felt in all his life. He was strapped into

a wheelchair, caught in a net, hanging from the ceiling fan. It was hopeless!

But just then William saw something dangling in front of his face. Something hanging from the ceiling like a lifeline. The pull-cord to switch the ceiling fan ON!

Suddenly, William had an idea.

There was no time to think it through: he *had* to get out into the street to help the Christmasaurus, and with his dad and Santa tied up it was all down to him!

He reached up and gave a hard tug on the cord. A *whirry-buzzing* sort of sound instantly filled the Trundles' living room as the blades of the ceiling fan started to spin. There was an ear-bursting screech from above as the fan struggled to turn with the weight of William and his chair hanging beneath it, so he pulled on the cord a few more times, selecting the highest, fastest, most powerful fan speed.

'William!' cried Mr Trundle. 'What are you doing? The fan will chop you to pieces!'

'Doooon't . . . woorreeeee . . . Daaaaaaaad!' yelled William as he was starting to spin round and round in the middle of the room. His escape plan was working!

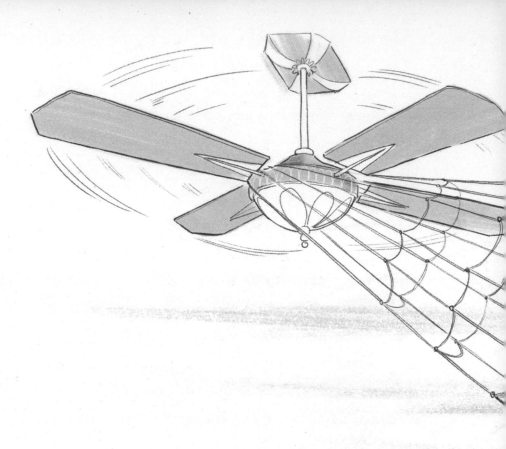

The ceiling fan started to gain momentum, picking up a tremendous amount of speed. As it got faster and faster, William started to feel the G-forces smushing and squishing his face in all sorts of ways it hadn't been smushed or squished in before.

'Hold on, son!' called Mr Trundle worriedly, watching

helplessly from the corner as William flew in great circles
round the living room.

William was now whizzing around so fast that to
everyone watching he just looked like a blurry smush
whooshing round and round and round – like some sort
of indoor Trundle tornado.

Suddenly there was a noise. A horrid, awful, tearing, ripping noise!

'William! The rope!' cried Santa, who had managed to spit his beard out of his mouth.

The rope holding the net to the ceiling was slowly being sliced by the blades of the fan. With each spin the rope was getting thinner and thinner. It wouldn't hold much longer!

'It's . . . oooookkaaaaay!' called William from somewhere within the spinning blur as he tried desperately not to throw up. 'Thiiiiiis . . . is . . . theeeeeee . . . plaaaaaaan . . . AAAAAARGH!'

The blade sliced through the final threads of rope as if they didn't even exist, and William found himself flying for the third time that night! He flew through the air, across the living room, over Santa's head, straight towards the window.

SMAAAAASH!

He crashed through the glass, landing with a great clatter in the snowy front garden underneath the heavy rope of the Hunter's net. Peering through the rope, he caught sight of the Hunter and Growler, stalking up the street in the direction from which the *roar* had come.

William tried to wriggle free from the ropes, but he was stuck. The ropes weren't just twisted and tangled. They were twangled! Twangled right around the wheels of his chair! It would take hours to untwangle it all, and the more he wriggled the more twangled the ropes seemed to get!

Suddenly William felt a rather odd sensation that everything was growing bigger. Or was he getting smaller? It was the same feeling he'd had on the rooftop just before falling down the chimney.

Santa was using his magic!

The ropes around William were now double the size . . . no . . . triple . . . Actually, they were ten times the size that they were, and so were the holes in the net! Just big enough for William to wheel himself through!

He quickly lifted one of the now huge, heavy ropes off his lap and over his head. He was free! He wheeled himself out of the enormous net and saw a very small Santa dramatically somersaulting through the now enormous broken window. An even smaller-looking Mr Trundle was running out of the even more enormous front door of their even more humongous wonky house!

'William!' the tiny, shrunken Mr Trundle called to his tiny shrunken son.

'Dad!' William cried as the massive world around them shrunk – or perhaps they all grew. Either way, everything was back to normal size in no more than three seconds.

William hugged his dad tighter than he'd ever hugged him before. He was so happy that he was safe and he still had his head!

'We've got to save the Christmasaurus!' Santa said urgently as another tremendous **ROAR** broke through the calm Christmas morning air.

The sun was still low in the sky, coating the white snow-quilted street in a fiery red glow. Santa, William and Mr Trundle hid behind the wonky hedge of the small front garden. They peeked over the top and saw the Hunter creeping down the middle of the snowy road, his deadly sniper rifle raised in his arms and his beady black eye stuck on to the telescopic sight. Growler was at his side, sniffing the fresh morning air, trying to pick up the scent of the Christmasaurus. Suddenly he let out a bark. He'd spotted something. The Hunter had spotted it too.

Right at the far end of the street, way off in the distance, was the unmistakable silhouette of a dinosaur.

'Look! It's the Christmasaurus!' whispered William worriedly. 'He came back!'

'He must have followed the sleigh. That silly dippy twozzle no-brained dinosaur! I told him to stay in the North Pole!' Santa cursed.

The sun was rising behind the Christmasaurus,

casting a long, dark, dinosaur-shaped shadow on the snow. A mighty **ROOOOAAAAR!**

came rolling down the street. The Christmasaurus was there all right!

'I need to put an end to this once and for all,' said Mr Trundle as he unexpectedly stood up and straightened his Christmas jumper.

'What are you doing, Dad?' William said, completely confused.

'Stay here, Willypoos.' And with those words, Mr Trundle marched fearlessly out into the street towards the Hunter.

'Dad! Stop! He'll shoot you!' cried William.

'No, he won't,' said Mr Trundle as he turned and looked William in the eye. 'He's my brother.'

CHAPTER THIRTY-ONE
GAME OVER

William's world was whizzing around him. Of all the impossible things he'd experienced that night, his father's last words were by far the most utterly, mind-blowingly unbelievable.

As he watched his dad step out into the street, standing in between the Hunter's raised rifle and the distant dinosaur, William searched his brain, searched his heart. Could that wretched man, standing like a statue carved out of pure evilness, really be his uncle?

'Hello, Huxley.' Mr Trundle's voice interrupted William's thoughts.

'Huxley? Now, that's a name I've not been called in a very long time,' sneered the Hunter, keeping his rifle raised.

'You've gone too far this time, Hux. Even by your standards,' said Mr Trundle.

'Well, I couldn't have done it without you, Robert,' said the Hunter with a sly grin. 'If it hadn't been for this beautiful Christmas card, I might never have found a way to catch Fatty Claus and his sleigh.' The Hunter reached inside his leathery coat pocket and pulled out the Trundles' traditional Christmas card with the photo of Mr Trundle and William on the front.

William gasped.

The Christmas cards they sent each year to their distant relatives! Great Nanna Joan, Second Cousin Sam . . . *Uncle H. Trundle.*

H. Trundle . . .

Huxley Trundle!

William suddenly knew it was true. All of it.

The Hunter was his uncle!

'Santa! It was my dad. He was the other little boy in the North Pole, wasn't he?' William asked.

Santa nodded.

It all became clear to William.

'That's why Dad loves Christmas so much. That's how he knows so much about it,' William realized.

'And why he's devoted his whole life since then to being good,' Santa said, and William remembered that his father had been banished from the North Pole.

'This has to end. Now. Put the gun down,' Mr Trundle said firmly as he stood blocking the Hunter's shot.

'If you think I won't pull this trigger because you're my brother, then you are in for a very nasty shock,' the Hunter said with evil honesty.

'It doesn't have to be this way, Hux. We're family.'

'Family? Pah!' spat the Hunter. 'I know what *family* means to you. I know what you're really after, what your pathetic Christmas cards and countless letters over the years have really been for – money. *MY* money! Slicing you out of my life all those years ago was the best thing I ever did.'

'You've got it all wrong, my brother,' replied Mr Trundle. 'I don't want the family money. I never have! Money causes more trouble than it's worth. That stuff has rotted your heart, Hux, but I want to buy it back with kindness.' And as Mr Trundle said those words he offered his hand for his brother to shake. 'A full heart is worth more than a full wallet.'

The Hunter paused. One eye was still glued to the sight of his rifle, while the other flickered momentarily to Mr Trundle's outstretched hand.

'You have precisely three seconds to get out of the way – or I'll *blast* you out of the way!' the Hunter said coldy as he closed his eye and took aim.

William knew he wasn't bluffing. 'Dad!' he called out.

'Three . . .' said the Hunter, his beady black eye

plastered to the sight. Mr Trundle didn't budge.

'Two . . . This isn't a game, little brother,' the Hunter warned.

Mr Trundle stayed put, defending the Christmasaurus. 'One.'

BANG!

The gunshot rang out, deafeningly loud as it tore through the street. It knocked Mr Trundle off his feet and sent him soaring through the air, before he landed in a heap on the pavement.

'DAD!' William screamed, tears exploding uncontrollably from his eyes.

The Hunter turned and faced him, the barrel of his smoking rifle pointing dangerously in his direction. 'Unless you want to say ta-ta to Santa Claus as well as your father tonight, you had better keep your mouth shut,' whispered the Hunter.

William continued crying silently, not taking his eyes from his father's body, lying motionless on the snow.

'Growler, it's time,' said the Hunter, as he turned back towards the shadowy dinosaur and crept up the street.

As soon as the Hunter and his mutt had walked a few metres away and were focused on their prey, William made a silent dash for his dad, closely followed by Santa. As William reached his father, tears filled his eyes so that he couldn't see. He sobbed and sobbed.

'Willypoos? Is that you?' whispered a soft, shaky voice.

'Dad! You're alive?' said William in amazement, quickly wiping away the tears.

Mr Trundle sat up on the pavement, looking completely confused.

'Yes . . . I suppose I am!' he said with surprise.

'Well, stuff my turkey!' Santa said in a jolly hushed

voice as he pointed at a smoking bullet hole in Mr Trundle's woolly Christmas jumper.

Mr Trundle placed his hand over his heart with a smile. Then he reached down inside the top of his jumper and pulled something out he had been wearing round his neck.

It was a thin, worn piece of brown leather, and when he reached the end William noticed that something was attached to it.

'The piece of reindeer antler!' William gasped in amazement, as the pointy, branchlike piece of horn popped out of Mr Trundle's jumper.

'I've worn it round my neck all these years,' Mr Trundle said, looking up at Santa.

He dangled the small piece of antler his evil brother had cut from the flying reindeer those many Christmases ago, and when Santa and William leant in closer they saw . . .

'The bullet!' William and Santa said at the same time. It was lodged deep inside the piece of antler.

'It saved my life!' said Mr Trundle.

'Well, there's one more life in need of saving right

now!' Santa said in a deeply troubled voice, staring up the street. Mr Trundle and William peeked out from their hiding place behind their neighbour's snow-covered car. They saw the Hunter silently slip a sleek bullet into his repulsive rifle, lift it to his bloodshot eyeball and release a puff of thick smoke from his pipe. Then they heard that awful, heart-stopping sound again:

BANG!

One single gunshot was all it took. It was violently loud as it *zoomed* down the street towards the shadowy dinosaur.

'NO!' William screamed.

But it was too late.

The Hunter hit his target.

The sun was gleaming, but there was no dinosaur silhouette any more. There was only a shadowy heap, lying very still in the distance where the dinosaur had been.

GAME OVER

'*YIPPEE! Yahoo! HOORAY!* It's mine. I did it! Did you see that shot, Growler, you silly old mutt? I shot him! I SHOT HIM! HA!' The Hunter screamed and cheered and celebrated with a vile dance in the middle of the street, whooping and waving at the sky.

As he danced his wicked celebration, light, fluffy snowflakes started descending from above.

William was crying. Santa was crying. Mr Trundle was crying. There was nothing they could have done to stop it. It was game over. The Hunter had won.

He had killed the Christmasaurus.

Chapter Thirty-two

FEATHERS

'**G**rowler, stay! Keep an eye on Fatty and the boy. Don't let them go anywhere – I'll deal with them in a minute. I'm going to fetch my prize,' said the Hunter, and Growler immediately turned his dirty, matted face towards the tearful trio, sobbing behind the car.

The Hunter puffed merrily on his pipe and whistled a little tune as he strutted proudly down the street.

'Foolish dinosaur. Coming back to save your friends, were you? Ha! It was all too easy!' he cackled at the motionless dinosaur-shaped lump in the shadows ahead,

whilst wafting away the irritating snowflakes that had begun falling on his hard, scarred, face.

Suddenly something got stuck in his mouth. It was soft and fluffy.

'*Ptui*' he spat. Then more of this odd falling fluff started brushing his face, getting in his eyes.

'What the devil is this?' he said, and then he suddenly realized something most peculiar.

They weren't snowflakes falling from the sky . . .

They were **feathers!**

'Feathers?' the Hunter said, waving them away from his face. They were falling as thick as a blizzard all around. The closer he got to the body of the dinosaur, the thicker this feather storm seemed to get. 'Is this some sort of trick?'

As the falling feathers cleared he could see the lifeless lump of the body he had shot.

'No, it can't be . . .' muttered the Hunter in disbelief.

Lying on the ground where he expected to see the Christmasaurus was William's beautiful stuffed dinosaur toy!

It was as close to a perfect replica of the Christmasaurus as you could get, slightly smaller, of course, but from a distance you would never have been able to tell the two apart – and the Hunter certainly couldn't, even through his super-zoom telescopic sight!

He marched over to it, with his rifle aimed at its perfectly stitched head.

'No!' he gasped as he gazed into two lifeless golden buttons staring up from the snow. There was now a large bullet hole in the toy dinosaur's side and its feathery stuffing was leaking out into the Christmas morning air and blowing away in the light breeze.

'But . . . but he *must* be here somewhere!' the Hunter whined. 'I heard him roar with my own ears! He must still be close!'

And he was.

As the Hunter stood cursing at his misfortune, screaming manically at the wounded stuffed dinosaur on the ground, something was creeping up behind him.

From the other end of the street, the crying crowd of criers quickly wiped away their tears as they saw something wonderful.

Something tremendous.

Something *ferocious*!

It was the Christmasaurus, but he looked different from how he'd ever looked before. More dinosaur-like.

Protective.

Fierce . . .

Hungry.

The Hunter spun on the spot to find himself standing in the looming shadow of the Christmasaurus. He was face to face with an angry dinosaur. For the first time in his life the Hunter was being *hunted*!

'W-w-wait just a clock tick!' the Hunter said nervously as he started backing away from the approaching dinosaur. 'I wasn't *really* going to hang you on my wall. This is all just . . . just . . . a misunderstanding . . .'

But as he spoke he was fiddling with something behind his back.

Click!

It was his rifle, and it was reloaded and ready to fire again!

In a flash, the Hunter swung round his deadly gun and aimed it straight at the Christmasaurus's head. The Hunter was fast, and before the Christmasaurus had a chance to react he placed his bloodshot eye on the telescopic sight and was ready to pull the trigger. He would not miss this time!

But as his finger tightened, something came hurtling through the air at tremendous speed.

It was a small, hard, perfectly made snowball, and it flew down the street towards the Hunter with such

incredible speed and accuracy that there was no way he could avoid being hit.

The unexpected ball of snow knocked the sniper rifle straight out of the Hunter's bony fingers before he could pull the trigger!

The Hunter looked up just in time to see a giant set of white, glistening, razor-sharp dinosaur teeth coming towards him . . .

CRUNCH!

GULP!

The Christmasaurus

The Hunter was gone.

The Christmasaurus swallowed him whole.

There was nothing left of that beastly evil man.

FEATHERS

The Christmasaurus let out a big, stinky

BuuuUUURP!

that stank of pipe smoke and money, and that was the last anyone ever saw of the Hunter.

Chapter Thirty-three
THE WONDERFUL THING ABOUT CHRISTMAS

'You're alive! YOU'RE ALIVE!' William cried as he came whizzing down the street as fast as his wheelchair could whizz him. He flung his arms round the Christmasaurus's neck and gave him the biggest hug. 'Thank you!' he said. 'You saved us! You came back and you saved us all!'

Mr Trundle came running down the street after William, his mouth hanging open in complete shock at the sight of the Christmasaurus.

'Dad. *This* is the Christmasaurus! He's my best friend!' William said.

'How do you do? Merry Christmas . . .' said Mr Trundle nervously.

'It's OK – he's perfectly safe! We visited the museum tonight, and he flew me all the way to the North Pole, and we met all the elves and ate magic candy cane and – well, it's been quite an adventure, really,' explained William. 'Where's Santa?'

Just then, Santa came flying down from the sky in his enormous sleigh and landed it in the street next to them.

'William, William, William! That was one incredible snowball you threw there. Perfect shape, perfect size, perfect throw, perfect timing! Well done, you!' Santa applauded.

'It wasn't me who threw that snowball,' said William.

Santa and Mr Trundle looked completely puzzled.

'What do you mean? If it wasn't you, dear lad, then who on earth was it?' asked Santa.

William hadn't actually seen who'd thrown the snowball, but there was only one person he knew who could throw something with such unbelievable accuracy. He turned his wheelchair round and pointed his finger towards that sad, un-Christmassy-looking house on their street. The only house without Christmas decorations.

'You can come out, Brenda! It's OK!' William called.

The little bush in the front garden gave a wobble and out popped the perfect golden blonde twirls of Brenda Payne.

'Well, well, well, who's this? I don't recall dropping into your house last night!' puzzled Santa.

'No, you wouldn't, Santa,' said William. 'This is Brenda Payne. She's on . . . *the other list*,' he whispered.

'Ooooooh,' said Santa. 'Awkward!'

'It's OK,' Brenda said nervously as she took tiny baby steps towards them. 'I deserve it,' she admitted, and William saw that little smile creep into the corner of her mouth as she gazed up at Santa, unable to look at anything other than the impossibly magical man in red.

The Christmasaurus stomped his feet in the snow and gave Santa and William a very stern look. They both knew what he was saying.

'Brenda, my dear, what you have done here tonight took courage and bravery. It showed that deep down you care, that you are kind, and that you have the ability to put others first. If those aren't the sorts of deeds that get a kid on the Nice List these days, then I don't know what are!' said Santa warmly.

'You mean – I'm . . . I'm *NICE*?' asked Brenda, sounding more surprised than anyone.

'Brenda Payne, I hereby declare that you are no longer on the Naughty List!' bellowed Santa in a very official-sounding tone.

Everyone cheered and whooped, and Brenda gave William a huge, squeezy hug.

'Well, William, Brenda, Mr Trundle, I think it's time for me to be going. It's Christmas morning and I really shouldn't be parking the sleigh in the middle of the street like this. Traffic wardens don't take any Christmas holidays, you know. I put them all on the Naughty List years ago,' explained Santa.

'But how did you know to come back?' William asked the Christmasaurus. 'How did you know we were in danger?'

The Christmasaurus shook his head.

'I don't think *that's* the reason he came back, William!' Santa said, as the Christmasaurus moved out of the way to reveal the remains of the stuffed toy dinosaur lying on the floor. 'You left your toy behind in the North Pole. I think he was just trying to bring it back to you!'

The Christmasaurus nodded, his tongue flapping happily out of his mouth.

'And it's a good job too, or we might all have ended up as heads above the Hunter's fireplace!' William exclaimed, and everybody burst out with laughter at the thought.

Then William noticed something red, white and scrummy reflecting the sunlight on the floor next to Stuffy.

'My piece of candy cane!' William cried, and scooped it up.

Only something was different. Something had changed!

As he turned it over in his hands, he saw that the writing that ran through it that had once said his name now said: **BOB TRUNDLE**.

William's eyes lit up with excitement.

'Does this mean . . .?' He looked hopefully up at Santa, who was smiling back down at him. 'That my dad is . . . ?'

'UN-BANISHED!' Santa boomed with a merry laugh, and William handed over the magical piece of North Pole protection confectionery into Mr Trundle's trembling hands.

'I don't know what to say!' gulped Mr Trundle with tears of happiness in his eyes.

'Say you'll come and visit!' said Santa.

Suddenly there was a loud **WOOF!** from behind them. They all turned to see Growler, the Hunter's dog, sitting in the snowy street, looking very lost and alone.

'Hmmm,' Santa said. 'I wonder if there might be some good in this dog after all?'

They all saw that something was different in the hound's eyes. Now that the Hunter was gone he looked happier, nicer. 'I wonder, Brenda, if *you* might be able to show him the love and kindness that you have shown here tonight?' Santa said.

As he spoke, the great shabby dog bounded over to Brenda, jumped up and gave her a big, wet, happy lick across her face.

'Santa, do you really mean it? I can keep him?' asked Brenda excitedly.

'Well, I believe I owe you a present. You are on the Nice List now, after all! As long as you promise to give him a happy home,' said Santa.

'Of course I will! I love him!' said Brenda, and she gave Growler the first hug he'd ever had, which seemed to melt away all the rottenness inside him.

The Christmasaurus let out a happy roar as William

wheeled himself round so that he was face to face with his dinosaur friend.

It was time to say goodbye – again.

'You can come and visit us whenever you want to. Just be sure to let Santa know first, OK?' said William, and the Christmasaurus nodded.

They hugged each other, and it was one of those hugs that only best friends give. Even though they didn't know when they would see each other again, they knew that a friend is for life, not just for Christmas.

'CHRISTMASAURUS!' Santa boomed. 'I do believe there's room for a certain dinosaur up front.'

He pointed to an empty harness at the front of the team of magnificent reindeer.

The Christmasaurus looked at the sleigh.

Then back at Santa with his wondrously icy blue eyes.

'Yes, you heard me correctly, you silly sausage. I've been flying this sleigh one man down for thirty years – or should I say one deer down! Now, do you want to pull the sleigh or not?' Santa said as the Christmasaurus bounced around with excitement. 'Come on, then!

Let's get you strapped up!'

The Christmasaurus leapt over and lined himself up proudly in front of the magnificent reindeer. Santa strapped the enormous sleigh-belled harness over his shoulders, and a sort of warm, magical tingle ran from the top of the Christmasaurus's head all the way down his blue snowflake-covered back to the tip of his tail! Santa took a step back and they all admired the Christmasaurus. He wasn't a reindeer. He was still different. But he was just as magnificent – maybe even more so.

'Let's go home!' Santa cried, and he jumped up into his sleigh and wound up the shiny, golden gramophone for the last time.

As William, Mr Trundle, Brenda and Growler watched the sleigh start to softly float on the music, a worried voice called out.

'Brenda!'

Miss Payne was scurrying towards them, dressed in spotty pyjamas and a flowery dressing gown, her prettiness hidden behind a look of panic and worry.

'I heard noises, gunshots and roars, and when I

looked, you'd gone, and . . . and . . .' Miss Payne froze on the spot. She had been so worried about her daughter that she hadn't noticed the unbelievably impossible sleigh floating over the street in front of them.

'Oh my!' she gasped when she saw it, completely mesmerized, entirely spellbound through and through.

William saw the sparkle of tears well up in her eyes and thought that maybe, just maybe, Miss Payne's heart might just have thawed completely.

'Merry Christmas!' Santa called as Mr Trundle, Miss Payne, William, Brenda and her new dog watched the sleigh glide over the snowy street, pulled by eight magnificent reindeer and a flying dinosaur, to the sound of Santa's booming singing voice.

As Santa glanced down from the sky above, William thought he caught a glimpse of that knowing smile he'd seen earlier that night. Suddenly, Santa pulled on the reins and the Christmasaurus made a hard turn to the right, guiding the sleigh directly over their heads.

William had to spin his wheelchair round to keep sight of them, but as he did he heard an awful, familiar sound.

Crunch!

'That's my foot!' cried Miss Payne.

As she jumped back, she slipped on the icy street. Just before she landed in a pile of snow, Mr Trundle caught her in his arms.

William was about to apologize when something stopped him. Just a feeling he got. Instead, he just watched as his dad helped Miss Payne to her feet.

'Thank you,' she said, looking a little embarrassed.

'Don't mention it,' said Mr Trundle.

There was a funny little pause and William noticed that, since helping Miss Payne to her feet, Mr Trundle hadn't let go of her hand.

'I'm Bob. Bob Trundle,' Mr Trundle said. 'I don't believe we've met.'

'Pamela,' Miss Payne replied.

'Well, Merry Christmas, Pamela!' said Mr Trundle with the same silly tip of his invisible top hat. William rolled his eyes, but this time Miss Payne didn't ignore him or cross the street to get away.

'Merry Christmas, Bob,' she said, and blushed.

Perhaps it was the magic of the music falling from Santa's sleigh like a blanket of snow, or maybe Mr Trundle was feeling particularly jolly as it was Christmas. Whatever the reason, William couldn't quite believe what happened next.

'Shall we?' Mr Trundle said, as he offered Miss Payne his arm to dance.

'Oh . . . I . . . er, I really don't usually dance . . .' spluttered Miss Payne nervously.

'Neither do I!' Mr Trundle said with a little chuckle, which made them both laugh.

She took his arm. And so, for the second time that Christmas, William saw his father happily dancing in the wintry air.

'This is turning into the best Christmas ever!' Brenda said as she stood next to William with her new pet. 'I never want it to end!'

'That's the wonderful thing about Christmas,' William said, as his dad spun Miss Payne beautifully over the snow. 'Every step you take away from last Christmas brings you one step closer to the next.'

THE END

ACKNOWLEDGEMENTS

Firstly, thanks to Shane Devries, whose incredibly magical illustrations have brought my story to life in ways I couldn't even have dreamed of.

Thanks to Michael Gracey; without you and your incredible vision we wouldn't have found Shane and we wouldn't have the most awesome-looking dinosaur on the planet. I can't wait for what's to come next for the Christmasaurus!

Thanks to my agent, Stephanie Thwaites, who was the first person to really take us seriously when Dougie and I wanted to write books about a pooping dinosaur. It's been a super-fun journey with you since that first meeting. Thank you for always being so awesome!

Thanks to Dougie for co-creating our pooping dinosaur, who inadvertently pooped out this one, and to Danny and Harry for injuring themselves, causing our tour to be postponed, which gave me more time to work on this book.

I cannot even begin to thank my editor, Natalie Doherty, enough. The whole editing process was so much fun and I learned so much from you. Thanks for pushing me to keep trying to make it better and better.

Thanks to the whole team of elves at Penguin Random House who have been so incredibly supportive and lovely to me for the last five or so years. There are a lot of you, so in the spirit of Christmas, here's a Nice List that you're all on (I've checked it twice): Amanda Punter, Francesca Dow, Jessica Jackson, Rosamund Hutchison, Andrea Bowie, Alice Broderick, Vanessa Jedrej, Hannah Bourne, Anna Billson, Emily Smyth, Mandy Norman, Samantha Stewart, Zosia Knopp, Camilla Borthwick, Maeve Banham, Susanne Evans, Emma Jones, Ceri Cooper, Sarah Roscoe, Kirsty Bradbury, Tineke Mollemans, Kat Baker, Becki Wells, Chris Wyatt and Claire Simmonds. Thanks to you all

Acknowledgements

for allowing me to write books. I love it so, so much and I hope to be writing many more for years to come – please!

I owe an incredible amount of thanks to Fletch. Your belief in me and your passion for this story have been the driving forces that made it a reality. Thanks for all the crazy chats about dreams that are probably impossible and ambitions that are quite certainly unachievable. Those chats never fail to inspire me and somehow we end up on these journeys where occasionally those impossible, unachievable things actually happen!

Thanks most of all to my wife, Giovanna, for being the inspiration to stop saying 'I want to write a novel' and actually getting off my bottom and writing a novel! Thank you for encouraging my obsession with Christmas rather than divorcing me because of it, and for generally putting up with my ways, but most importantly for giving me my biggest inspiration of all: our two boys. Buzz and Buddy, this book is for you both.

Lastly, I want to say a HUGE thanks to the whole team at WhizzKidz. When I first decided to write a story about a young wheelchair user, I had no idea of the responsibility I was taking on. Your help, advice, stories and what you do on a daily basis is so inspiring, and I couldn't have done this without your support. I truly hope I've written something that will make wheelchair users proud and perhaps open the eyes of non-wheelchair users – the way you opened mine. Thank you.

ABOUT Whizz-Kidz
move a life forward

The story of Whizz-Kidz started with a bloke in a bike shop.

It was 1989, and our founder, Mike Dickson, was at work in his shop when he saw a girl in a wheelchair looking up at a bike light on the shelf above her. Mike asked if he could help, but the girl politely replied, 'No thanks, I can reach it myself,' pushed a button on her powered wheelchair and rose up to pick the light off the shelf.

It was at that moment that Mike understood the difference the right wheelchair can make to a child's life. Because to that little girl, that small action – getting something off a high shelf – meant something far bigger. It meant independence.

Mike set out to run the London Marathon and raise enough money to pay for a single powered wheelchair for a child who needed it. By the time he crossed the finish line, he'd raised £9,000 for a girl with cerebral palsy. One year later, Whizz-Kidz was born.

Since then, Whizz-Kidz has transformed the lives of more than 20,000 disabled children, providing them with life-changing mobility equipment to give them the best possible start in life.

Today, we do so much more than providing equipment to young disabled people; our youth clubs, wheelchair skills training, residential camps and work placements each contribute to helping young disabled people make friends, have fun, learn life skills and, ultimately, achieve their true potential.

We still have a long way to go, and many thousands of children are still waiting for the right equipment to give them freedom, independence and hope. But we are extremely proud of all we have achieved, and we are incredibly grateful to all of our supporters – including Tom – who have made our achievements possible.

Together, we'll continue working to achieve our vision that all disabled children's lives are full of fun, friendship and hope for an independent future. Just like any other kid's. **www.whizz-kidz.org.uk**

TOM'S TOP 10 THINGS ABOUT CHRISTMAS!

(NARROWED DOWN FROM 1,000)

 1   **The music!** Christmas songs rule. Full stop. Is it just me, or is 'I Wish It Could Be Christmas Every Day' the most relatable lyric of all time? Oh . . . it is just me.

 2   **Food, and lots of it.** I love everything about festive food. Even food I don't like – give it a Christmassy name and some magical packaging and it's in my shopping basket. Rename mixed nuts 'The Festive Mix' and SOLD! What even is a figgy pudding? Who cares! Nom nom nom.

 3   **Christmas movies.** We all know the ones I'm talking about. *Elf*, *Home Alone* (1 AND 2), *White Christmas*, *Miracle on 34th Street* . . . The list goes on and on and on. And let's not forget *Die Hard*.

The Snowman. *The Snowman* deserves to be listed on its own. I'm talking about both the book and the film. I have loved it since I was a little boy, and watching my son Buzz fall in love with it last Christmas and asking me to lift him up so that he could fly like the Snowman was an incredible moment.

TV adverts. I know what you're thinking. 'Who in their right mind gets excited about TV adverts? ME, that's who. Companies have been majorly upping their game these last few years. Monty the penguin was quite possibly the best ad of all time. I cried ugly tears.

Christmas Eve. I don't care that I'm in my thirties, I still get excited on Christmas Eve. It's by far the most magical night of the year and I remember exactly how it felt when I was a kid. I'm loving the fact that I get to experience it again through my own kids now.

7 Friends and family. It goes without saying that it's the time of year you make that extra effort to see those people you don't see as often as you should. When I think back on all my favourite Christmas memories, they're filled with my family or my friends – so I guess they deserve to be on the list.

8 **Christmas dinner.** I'm listing this separately from the other festive food because this meal is the ultimate. I've been in charge of the big meal for the last few years and, although I had a disaster with the gravy a while back, on the whole I think I've got pretty good at it. Of course you have to make a few practice meals in the weeks/months leading up to it, just to be safe.

9 **Street lights.** Our local high street has used the same Christmas lights for at least the last ten years, probably longer. They aren't anything special really, but that doesn't stop them from filling me with Christmas awesomeness the moment they are switched on. I always drive the long way home in December just so I get to see them. One year they tested them out in the summer in the middle of the night and I managed to get a sneaky look at them early. I was happy.

10 Last but not least, fake Christmas trees. Wait – did I just say fake? Yes, you read that right. Believe it or not, I'm pretty sure I have a mild allergy to Christmas trees (yes, that makes me very sad). It doesn't affect me badly, but having a real one in the house for over a month has caused me some serious issues. So I am REALLY grateful to whoever thought up the idea of fake Christmas trees. We've had the same one for as long as we have lived in our house, and even though it's looking a little shabby these days it wouldn't be Christmas without it.

(I still risk the allergy and sometimes have a small real tree in the kitchen . . . can't help myself.)

ELVES' SONG BOOK

The elves have got in a bit of a pickle.

Find the right rhyme or change it a little . . .

THE CHRISTMASAURUS HATCHES

'What type of dinosaur?'

'What's its _____?'

'Is it dangerous?'

'Or is it _____?'

'If it's a girl can we call her _____?'

'I think it's a boy! Look, he's got a _____!'

RHYME BOX

TAME   THINGY   GINNY   NAME

THE NIGHT BEFORE
THE NIGHT BEFORE CHRISTMAS

It's the night before the night before Christmas,
The worst night of the year.
There's far too much to do,
And it fills us up with _____.
It doesn't look like we'll make it
But we've brought this on ourselves,
So if Christmas doesn't come,
You can blame the North Pole _____.

It's the night before the night before Christmas,
And we're busier than ever before.
There are toys up to our _____,
And our hands and feet are sore.
But you don't hear us complaining –
We sing our troubles away,
Whilst saddling up the _____
To the still-not-ready sleigh!

It's the night before the night before Christmas,
No time for toilet breaks.
We've got microscopic fingers
So we might make some _____ .
But as long as the job gets finished,
And Santa gets on his way,
We'll be happier than the kiddies
Getting toys on _____!

RHYME BOX

EYEBALLS   MISTAKES   ELVES
CHRISTMAS DAY   REINDEER   FEAR

SANTA'S SONG FOR
THE CHRISTMASAURUS

'My wondrous little North Pole elves,
You must congratulate _____
For I believe beyond a doubt
A miracle has come about.
It's sitting right here on the floor
Looking like no other _____.'

'Another year you've served me well,
Through good times and the tough as well.
But I shall not forget the night
An egg was dug up from the ice.
And here he sits, this nameless _____ ,
With such fantastic festive features
That there is just one name for him –
Come one, come all, come hear me sing . . .
This Christmas dinosaur before us
Shall henceforth be known as the _____!'

RHYME BOX

CREATURE
YOURSELVES
CHRISTMASAURUS
DINOSAUR

I Ho, Ho, Hope It's Santa

I heard a noise on the rooftop!
It made my heart so jump!
The stomp of boots and the clop of hooves
Went clippedy, clippedy, clump!

Oh, I heard a noise on the rooftop!
I wonder what it was . . .
I really ho, ho, hope it's Santa Claus!

I heard a noise on the rooftop!
It sounded like a sleigh . . .
I went to bed on Christmas Eve,
and now it's Christmas Day!

Oh, I heard a noise on the rooftop!
I wonder what it was . . .
I really ho, ho, hope it's Santa Claus!

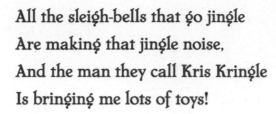

All the sleigh-bells that go jingle
Are making that jingle noise,
And the man they call Kris Kringle
Is bringing me lots of toys!

Oh, I heard a noise on the rooftop!
Now I can't sleep because
I really ho, ho, hope it's Santa . . .
Ho, ho, ho, ho, hope it's Santa . . .
Really ho, ho, hope it's Santa Claus!